BRIAN FRANCE

CLASH OF THE KINGDOMS

THE EPIC BATTLE BETWEEN THE SUPERNATURAL FORCES OF GOOD AND EVIL

WSP
WILD SIDE PUBLISHING
real stories. real hope.

Published by Brian France, in association with
Wild Side Publishing, PO Box 33, Ruawai 0549, New Zealand
wildsidepublishing.com

Cover design & text layout, Janet Curle | wildsidepublishing.com

Cataloguing in Publication Data:
Title: Clash of the Kingdoms

ISBN: 978-0-473-50563-9 (pbk)
ISBN: 978-0-473-50564-6 (ebook)

First published under the title *Against the Gates of Hell* (ISBN 9781434313102)
Revised version, *Clash of the Kingdoms*, with a new final chapter.

Subjects: Inspiration, Spirituality, Body Soul Spirit, Fantasy, Supernatural, Religion, Christian Theology, Angelology & Demonology, Christian Fiction

International listing January 2020 ingramspark.com
First New Zealand printing February 2020 yourbooks.co.nz

ACKNOWLEDGEMENTS

I wish to acknowledge a number of people who encouraged me and helped as this book was written.

The late evangelist, Bill Subritzky, had for many years inspired me with a ministry of deliverance that showed the reality of the casting out of demons and prayer for the healing of sickness. His affirmation of the book's content has meant a great deal to me and I have been most grateful for his friendship and support.

Some years ago, Jackie Pullinger allowed me the privilege of working with her and the St Stephen's Society in Hong Kong. I am grateful for her wonderful Christian ministry that truly "sets the captives free" from the bondage of drug addiction. My time with her ministry opened my eyes to what Christian ministry could be, and helped to sow the seeds for the writing of this book. Also, I am deeply appreciative of the foreword that Jackie has written for *Clash of the Kingdoms*.

I'd also like to thank Bernadette Soares, without whose generosity, this book would not have been re-published.

ENDORSEMENTS

"This is one of my favourite books of all time. I am a huge *Lord of the Rings* fan, and *Clash of the Kingdoms* is the supernatural equivalent, in a nutshell. Brian has brilliantly woven true events of history, as told in the Bible, about the fall of Satan and the redemption of mankind, into a thrilling page-turner with the power to challenge a generation. Brian France's way with words, spiritual insight and tactical warfare skills honed as a British Platoon Commander during "The Troubles" in Northern Ireland make for a breath-taking and totally engrossing read. A rare and powerful book indeed."

Janet Balcombe, author *The Wild Side* and *Radical Lives 1 & 2*

CONTENTS

FOREWORD

I first met Brian some 30 years ago when he came to Hong Kong to take part in the work of the St Stephen's Society, for a 2½ month period. Since that time, he has seen evidence of signs and wonders in many Christian ministries, such as ours, and this book is the fruit of some of his spiritual journeying.

Of course I knew the end of this story from the beginning. But once I started this amazing book I could not put it down. Full of guts, gore and glory, it tells the history of the world and that which is to come, from a unique perspective—that of angels and demons.

I am not a fan of Christian books, but this is one I would unreservedly recommend to anyone, including those who are not yet believers in the God of Creation. It will grip you and should throw you back to the source—the Bible. That is my measure of spiritual literature; whether it gives one a thirst to discover more of the truth of Scripture. Obviously, it is part fantasy and wonderfully embellished, but nevertheless, rather credible. I personally had one or two theological leaps and are still enjoying making biblical landfall on some of the scenes.

We ignore the enemy at the peril of our own lives. "Deliver us from evil," said Jesus, so it must be critical. This book highlights why the evil one became so when he was also created an angel. Thus, it contains lessons for us all, in an age where worship has been revived and glorified in our Christian communities.

This is a big tale. The angels are huge, beautiful and number in hosts. The demons are large too, and powerful. There are battles upon battles. The greatest battle of all has been won on the cross, so for us followers of Jesus, there is much comfort in the knowledge that we are not only fighting with the aid of our Saviour, but with myriads of mostly unseen angelic beings. May it bring encouragement to all who are still in the war, and for the battles yet to be fought?

Jackie Pullinger
Author, *Chasing the Dragon*
St Stephen's Society
Hong Kong

C1

WAR IN HEAVEN

The atmosphere was tense with aggression and hatred as it always was when Satan was close by. The fear, by which he controlled his demons, was physically tangible and sat as an oppressive force over them all. His visible anger and irritation, being held in check but leaving no doubt, that they were experiencing the calm before the storm.

In his form as the Great Red Dragon, stood Satan dribbling smoke from his nostrils; a sure sign that his internal fire was kindled. His great scaly tail wove menacingly from side to side, graphically illustrating the level of rage and irritation residing within him. His demonic presence commanded the attention of his subordinate demons. With his bellowing voice being heard by all, as he yelled at his demon warriors, *"You will kill and destroy all who oppose me or I will destroy you"*, Satan snarled, as he bullied and growled at the demons before him. *"Know that I will reign supreme, and if all of you have to die to maintain me as Lord Satan, then so be it, for you are expendable. I care nothing for your lives; you are scum and I loathe your very existence!"*

He belched red and green flames as he spoke, shambling

up and down before his assembled forces. His great tail flailing from side to side, as anger and hatred poured from his being.

The army of demons with their gruesome, reptilian features, black helmets and formidable weapons, stood before Satan their commander-in-chief. Their swords and battle-axes presented a challenge of horrendous proportions to the angels opposing them. Every demons' evil intent was apparent from the aggression they emitted and could be heard from their grunts, as they struck their shields in a rhythmic challenge, to the angels facing them.

The Archangel Michael, captain of the hosts of Heavens' armies, stood before his angel warriors arrayed in their battle formations. Facing this formidable demonic foe, every angel knew they must fight courageously and die, if necessary, to prevent an evil and eternal spiritual abyss from opening up and swallowing them and everything they valued.

A young demon in the front rank of Satan's forces was terrified at the thought of conflict and death. With a trembling voice full of fear, said he did not want to die and would prefer to leave. The sound of his voice had barely died away, when Satan reacted. With bulging red eyes, which looked as though they might burst from their sockets, he turned to face the frightened wretch who had dared to speak, he growled dangerously, *"Afraid to fight and die are you? So die, you shall!"*

A streak of orange flame leapt from the Great Dragon's mouth, with a crack that sounded like a high voltage discharge and arced towards the demon. He screamed as it hit him and was instantly engulfed in flames. His screams intensified as his body burned and was consumed by the fire. In a few seconds all that remained was a small mound of carbon ash and the smell of sulphur.

The effect the execution of this young demon had on the rest of the demons was electric. They opened their mouths and out poured a cacophony of speech, born of fear, "Don't kill me Lord Satan, I will always serve you!" Others exclaimed amongst the general hubbub of shouting and noise, "You are my Lord and I worship you Satan. My life is yours and I live for you, don't kill me!"

Satan restored order by standing on his massive hind legs, raising his nostrils vertically and roaring, whilst emitting a volcano-like eruption of flame and smoke. Silence quickly ensued, and then he spoke in a loud, low growl, "I have told you what to do! You will destroy and kill those who oppose me, and I will have your obedience. You will obey me and kill - or be killed. You are to ravage my enemies and impart to them death and destruction. Do you understand!?" To reinforce his point, he screamed at them, *"Death and destruction! Death and destruction!"*

The cry of, "Death and destruction," was taken up by all the demons as they drew their swords and brandished them above their heads. Screaming at the top of their voices they worked themselves into a frenzy of aggression and hatred. Satan saw what was happening and ground his teeth in satisfaction whilst growling deep in his throat and firing flames of encouragement over the heads of his demon army.

"Death and destruction!! Death and destruction!! Death and destruction!" Their frenzy deepened as they shouted, stamped their feet and brandished their swords and battle-axes. They

fed off each other's growing momentum to kill and destroy, as they gave free reign to their insatiable appetite for violence. They voiced their desire by screaming their war cry, with all the power with which their lungs were capable.

The angels saw and heard all that was happening and also heard Michael's order to regroup. They closed ranks and reshaped their formations, their regiments forming a hollow square and within each regiment the battalions, brigades and companies occupied their own space, with their commanding officers taking up their positions before them. Michael spoke to them in a loud clear voice, "This day corruption has entered this most holy place, but we must stand firm and uphold the values of Heaven. Our loyalty and devotion to the Lord must never be in doubt and the perfection of His kingdom will be re-established."

He continued, "We are angels who inhabit the realms of glory and our courage and skill, as members of the army of the Lord of Hosts, is about to be tested. Today we will fight under Heaven's banner, with holiness and righteousness as our breastplate, in the sure conviction that we will defeat the Lord's enemies and cleanse His Kingdom of all unrighteousness. Be bold; be brave, for the Lord your God is with you".

Every angel listened intently to Michael's words and felt their heart strengthened. None noticed the dark mass that had been moving silently around behind them, until the demon hoards struck without warning at their rearmost ranks.

Taken by surprise, many angels were cut down where they stood, by black swords they never saw. The attackers immediately withdrew through their own ranks, leaving the dead and wounded where they fell. The front rank of demons was now massive dragons, that breathed fire, who at their leader's command, spewed tongues of flame deep into the ranks of the angels. As they did so they moved their scale-covered heads from side to side, increasing their coverage and inflicting maximum damage. The result was a scene of carnage and confusion, as some angels were consumed by fire and others tried to escape the flames.

Satan pressed home his advantage, by ordering the dragons to withdraw and commanding two battalions of scorpions to attack. As the dragons withdrew, the scorpions raised their venomous stings, arching them over their backs until they were positioned in front of their heads. Their battalion commander gave the order to charge and they moved forward as one mass through the smoke, trampling the dead and wounded underfoot as they struck the ranks of angels in their path.

Having recovered from the suddenness and surprise of the initial onslaught, the angels had, on the orders of their company commanders, regrouped and were ready to face this new demonic threat. On the command, *"SHIELD COVER!"* the front rank of warriors dropped to one knee, while positioning their shields in front of them. The second row leaned forward and interlocked the bottom of their shields with the tops of the shields of those kneeling and angled them back at 45 degrees. The angels in the third row quickly raised their shields above their heads and interlocked with the second row of shields. The next three rows of angels did the same, forming a defensive barrier that protected all the angels enclosed within it.

Four battalions of angels moved to left and right and

advanced down the flanks of the attacking scorpions. The forward momentum of the scorpions brought them into contact with the shield defenses, which absorbed the initial impact of their stings and held firm. The scorpions hissed loudly in frustration at their attack failing, their tails swung from side to side and their stings pounded the shields with little effect.

The angels on the scorpions' flanks now charged at them from the sides where the stings could not get to them. Some angels concentrated on putting out the scorpions' eyes whilst others sliced off their stings with razor sharp swords. The scorpions' battalion commander saw that the engagement was lost and ordered them to withdraw.

Satan was at the rear of his forces screaming abuse and obscenities at them for their failures. His frustration was extreme and only heightened as he realised that the archangel Michael had ordered a pincer movement that threatened to surround his forces.

The cunning of Satan now came to the fore as he quickly planned a defensive strategy. Bellowing at the top of his voice he ordered his foot soldiers into a hollow circle with the remaining scorpions surrounding them and a large circle of dragons forming the first line of defense on their outside. He quickly moved to the safest place at the centre of the innermost circle and from there he would order them to fight to the death if necessary, in the preservation of his own life.

The angels had now completed their pincer movement and surrounded the demons. Michael's warriors were at the front of his forces with the other angels behind them. They faced the fire breathing dragons resolutely, seeing them to be a fearsome foe but also knowing that they had the Lord on their side.

Michael again rose above them and prayed a prayer of blessing over them, "Holy and Living God, I ask for your protection to cover each of your servants here this day. May we be valiant in your service and in the doing of your will? Give us the courage to be bold for you and the skill to vanquish those who stand against your rule and reign. May your blessing be upon us? Amen."

Again the order, *"Shield cover!"* rang out and with practiced precision the front six ranks of warrior angels formed their shields into a protective barrier against the fire of the dragons. As they advanced towards the huge monolithic beasts, the commander of the dragons gave the order that was to bring flame and heat to bear on the ranks of angels that were closing for battle. *"Target! Angels to your front. Range 100; heat intense; prepare to spew fire."* Each dragon opened its mouth wide and sucked in a massive amount of air, filling their lungs and awaited the next part of the fire control order that came after a brief pause, *"Fire!"*

Each dragon now forced the air in its lungs out through its broad nostrils and as it did so massive orange flames tinged with black smoke poured forth. The heat produced was intense and had it not been for the barrier provided by the shields, it would have incinerated the angels at whom it was aimed.

Behind their shields the angels could feel the heat but continued their advance. As they closed the gap between the dragons and themselves, the dragons intensified their fiery defense by increasing the quantity and temperature of the flames... the roar was loud in the angels' ears. As they did so, more and more heat was reflected off their shields and back into the dragons' faces. The head and body of the dragon nearest to the flames started to smolder; his green leathery wings were the first to catch fire. The fire spread to his body and he burst into flames with a roar, as the combustible materials within him ignited. He exploded spreading burning liquid and body parts over the dragons on either side. Their agony and distress was immediately apparent by the screams of pain and roars of rage that came from them.

Some of the burning material fell on the scorpions behind the dragons and a melee began as the pain of their burns caused them to move about in an attempt to avoid the falling, flaming debris. They broke ranks and charged around screaming and hissing, as their burns spread and their pain and distress increased. Two more dragons exploded and the hot burning material from their bodies showered upon the scorpions.

The demons surrounding Satan at the centre of their defensive circle were becoming more and more alarmed and agitated as they observed what was happening. Their ironclad feet were trampling some of their number who were closest to the scorpions. Satan was determined to retain control of his forces. He bellowed at them in rage for their lack of discipline under fire and their inadequate performance in battle, "You incompetent oafs; you absolute imbeciles! Look at the danger you are placing me in! Scorpions advance and close that gap – move, you idle loafers!"

To give his words emphasis, he fired a strong bolt of flame across the tails of the scorpions facing the space where the defunct dragons had been. They quickly moved forward into the gap and lined up with the remaining dragons. Two of the scorpions were in obvious pain and their burns continued to smoke but the graphic illustration of the young demon, which Satan had incinerated, was still fresh in their minds and they hissed in pain but held their positions.

The advance of the angels now brought them to within a swords length of their enemy. They were right under the noses of the dragons and scorpions with the shield cover continuing to provide excellent protection. Their primary target was Satan himself, but to get to him they would have to penetrate the ranks of the demons that surrounded and shielded him; hand-to-hand fighting would be the only way to do it.

A huge, golden, glistening angel who was the commander of the battalion providing shield cover, now shouted in a loud voice, **"Raiding company, ready! Prepare to advance...** *Advance!"*

Simultaneously all the angels in the front rank raised their shields above their heads. As they did so the fourth, fifth and sixth ranks of angels moved forward under cover of the shields over them and through the ranks of the angels in front of them. Their swords were drawn ready for battle. As they cleared the front rank the shield cover came down again.

Using their wings the angels rose high above the dragons and scorpions, intending a fast attacking descent deep into the centre of the demons defending Satan, their principle goal being to take him captive.

To assemble their attack formation the angels regrouped several hundred feet above the enemy. Looking down they could see the battle in progress and were able to assess the strength of Satan's forces. The dragons and scorpions were his first line of defense and then came giant poisonous spiders and enormous reptilian creatures, that had the appearance of crocodiles but with a mouth full of razor sharp teeth at either end of their bodies. After them, came at least twenty rows of armour-plated demons dressed in black from head to toe and armed with long saw-edged swords and battle hatchets; their hideous faces obscured and protected by steel visors.

The next defensive layer was Satan's personal bodyguard, commanded by General Zenuk, a massive and fearsome demon-warrior. He was squat in stature being nearly as broad as he was tall. His black leather armour with steel inserts covered his chest, elbows and knees giving his body superb protection. He wore a thick black leather helmet complete with a slotted steel visor, that protected his head and face, making him almost impervious to attack. He was totally devoted to his Master Satan.

The bodyguards under the command of General Zenuk carried a large rectangular shield, emblazoned with a roaring red dragon and every one of them carried a mace and chain. They were also armed with an ugly curved dagger secured in their waistband. Each had four faces enabling them to look in four directions at once and they rode an eight-legged creature that resembled a cobra snake. The legged-snakes opened and closed their mouths constantly revealing large pairs of poisonous fangs and long forked tongues, that flashed in and out tasting the air and looking for whom they might attack.

The raiding party numbered some six thousand angels who now adopted a 'funnel' battle-formation with a large open circle of warriors leading. The tail of the funnel comprised a 'capture-net company' whose task was to physically ensnare and restrain Satan, in a net designed to hold him and in which he would be imprisoned and transported for judgment.

When the angel commanding the raiding party saw that his forces were correctly positioned he ordered them to attack. The entire formation moved downwards as a synchronized body, with wings beating and swords drawn ready to do battle. The 'capture-net company' flew with their large circular net open and ready for use.

From the ground, they appeared as a gold and silver funnel that glistened and gleamed with the only sound being made by their gossamer wings. The angels forming the funnel's opening, aimed to completely surround Satan. As they neared the ground his bodyguard saw their approach and rose to meet them.

Satan was beside himself with anger and indignation that he should be put at risk and under threat in this way. His great tail swept from side to side as he roared orders at those charged with his safety. He blasted flame skyward from his cavernous jaws and cursed the angels descending towards him.

Holding their positions, the angels watched as the demons of Satan's bodyguard closed with them. They had never seen such a horrific enemy and the sky was soon full of black figures on their cobras, clashing with silver and golden angels. Swords of light flashed and parried against mace and chain as a pitched battle ensued. Twisting and turning the opposing forces strove to gain the advantage and the shouted commands of leaders could be heard above the noise of battle.

It soon became apparent that it required three angels to

engage one bodyguard comprising demon and snake; two angels dealing with the vicious fangs and lashing tongue of the cobra, whilst the third fought the armour covered demon.

Casualties were soon occurring on both sides with dead and wounded falling to the ground, gaps in the opposing forces began to appear. All the while the angels pressed downwards and onwards toward their goal. Soon they were fighting on the main battlefield with the dragons and scorpions and were hard-pressed on all sides, until a tremendous roar was heard as the angels being held in reserve moved forward to join the battle.

The scene was now one of total engagement as every warrior-angel and every demon fought for their lives and for the victory each knew they must win. The battlefield was a mass of clashing weapons, smoke, blood, wounded and dying angels and demons; with no mercy being asked and none being given. Each combatant giving everything they had and being very aware of the consequences of defeat.

The warrior angels whose task it was to capture Satan, were closing in on their quarry as they fought their way through the cobra-mounted demons defending him. They had perfected their technique for dealing with this menace and in teams of three were now expediently dispatching them. With only two ranks of the bodyguard remaining, the angels with the net, swooped down covering the Great Red Dragon and felt the force of his strength as he thrashed and fought against being contained within it. Two mighty angels of enormous size and stature pulled the ends of the net tightly together ensuring there would be no escaping from it.

Now, from the very rear ranks of the angels came several

hundred with powerful wings, who had been kept for the special task of lifting Satan above the still raging battle. They each grasped a portion of the net and on Michael's command rose a hundred feet above the battle ground and maintained their position; hovering with powerful wings beating to support Satan's massive weight. Michael shouted above the noise of battle, "Demons, your leader has been captured, look and see. He is our prisoner!"

When Michael finished speaking the noise of battle began to subside as demons looked upwards and saw their leader entangled in the net. Satan was quite helpless, lying on his back unable to move, a pathetic sight with all the bluff and fight gone from him. Michael continued, "You must now surrender to the servants of the Living God and be judged by Him. Put down your weapons and there will be no more killing this day."

Michael's own body language now followed the desire in his heart for he wanted the battle to cease. He raised his sword high in the air and turned it point down, placing its tip between his outspread feet. He then put one hand on top of the other covering the heel of his sword and waited. There was no mistaking his absolute command of the situation, his whole being exuded authority and confidence.

The movement of battle, the clash of weapons and the hubbub of noise slowly subsided, until there was absolute silence. Angels and demons stood toe to toe in the positions in which they had been fighting. Even the cobras and crocodiles were quite still; the remaining dragons were also static with wispy smoke dribbling from their nostrils. Every eye was looking towards Michael with a defeated and bound Satan within their field of vision.

The silence was broken by a large and sinister figure clad entirely in black, the commander of Satan's bodyguard. It was General Zenuk's deep gruff growling voice that was now heard across the battlefield, "My Lord Satan is taken: I have failed in my duty. My life is worth nothing."

As Michael had done, Zenuk raised his sword high but instead of placing the tip between his feet, he put it into his midriff and instantly fell forward onto it. He made barely a sound as the sword ran through him and came out his back as he pitched onto his face, quite dead.

Zenuk's actions broke the impasse and the fighting spirit of every demon. In an almost synchronized movement their swords and other weapons were dropped to the ground. The battle was over and their surrender complete.

C2

THE FALL OF LUCIFER

The Archangel Michael stood with his wings furled and an arm resting lightly upon the shoulder of his friend Loyola. The two angels had survived the battle and were now physically weary and drained emotionally. Although unscathed by the battle both had been deeply affected by the betrayal that caused the conflict. Loyola was the first to speak, "It's hard to believe what has happened and I realise that our lives will never be the same. How could Lucifer do what he did? It's beyond my understanding!" Michael shifted his position to face Loyola and spoke quietly, "It's because of our free will that such things can happen. Like us all, Lucifer could decide things for himself and controlled his own destiny but I would never have thought rebellion was in his heart."

Michael's thoughts went back to the beginning as his mind thought through what had happened. It had started so well when all of God's angels presented themselves before His throne to worship and honour Him. They had come from every portion of the heavens, and every part of creation and numbered thousands upon thousands and ten thousands upon ten thousands. A countless assembly of angelic beings, their hearts full of praise and worship, with hands raised in adoration, voices in exaltation.

The sound of their singing was beautifully harmonious, with deep resonating notes that were reminiscent of the bass pipes of a massive organ enfolding the most spectacular sunset. Their voices spanned the full musical range from the deepest bass up into the highest galleries. Their ascending bell-like tones were as beautiful as the sweetest birdsong. The intricate fabric of their worship encompassed sounds that could be likened to cascading waterfalls embracing the softness of twilight.

Angelic voices were raised in praise and worship with no clearly defined source or point of origin. It was as though the sound emanated from the infinite depths of eternity, whilst embracing the present moment and the entirety of creation. Within their song was a singleness of purpose, to give glory and honour to the God they adored.

Their singing rose and fell in acoustic perfection as crescendo and diminuendo followed each other. Their worship combined into a timeless giving of the very core of themselves to the One who was their Lord. He had designed and created them and they worshiped Him with every part and portion of their being.

Their unity bound them together. The purity of their intentions and the holiness of their hearts combined to provide a glowing radiance that emanated from each angel. It formed a halo of white crystal light, which surrounded the assembly and provided a confirming mark of their purity.

In the very centre of this worshipping throng was the

manifest presence of the Father. The perfection of His holiness established across the universe, the power and warmth of His infinite love flowing to all creation; being joyously received and wholeheartedly returned.

The status of the Father was "Absolute Majesty," with the crown of his sovereignty symbolizing his eternal throne. The Father's holiness, beyond comprehension by finite beings, but His grace allowing a measure of understanding to dwell in the minds of those He had created.

The textures and colours of the Father's presence were almost incomprehensible. The rich, deep, timeless hews of integrated perfection; embracing the sparkle of diamond points of uncut shafts of light. All blended with the dancing molecules of sapphire crystals on a bed of velvet softness. The golden texture of Kingship combined with the emerald and turquoise of Majesty. The sparkling radiance of His glory enveloped His throne and His royal presence. Covering all was a depth and sacrificial in tenor and all-embracing by intention. It could not be seen and yet was so tangible that it could be felt, experienced and received.

Within this kingdom setting He provided the single focus for worship and adoration. The heart of angels was filled to overflowing with love for their Sovereign Lord. The freedom of their wills surrendered completely to their desire to worship the Living God.

All of Heaven's angelic host were there. Fiery seraphim with their six silky wings, cherubim with their gift of knowledge and the warrior angels of Michael's armies, their swords gleaming. There were small and large angels, messengers, helpers and the angels of death. In a circle surrounding the Royal Presence were the twenty-four elders seated, on their thrones with golden crowns on their heads. Their robes were white and spotless.

Over the Father's throne was the most magnificent rainbow and before it a sea of crystal glass. From the throne came sights and sounds that signified His power, flashes of lightning and crashes of thunder. Before the throne stood seven lit torches, representing the seven spirits of God and around it were four of Heaven's most amazing creatures. One had the appearance of a lion and another that of a bull, another looked like a man, and yet another like a flying eagle. Each of these creatures had six wings and many eyes and they sang constantly of the Lord's holiness and extolled his glory, giving him praise, thanks and honour.

Close to the throne of God was the mightiest angel of all. In all his magnificence stood Lucifer, the "Bearer of the Light". His being was majestic and his proportions perfect, his stature awe-inspiring. As he drew himself up to his full height and raised his arms the jewels and gold that adorned him gleamed and sparkled in the light of his wisdom and holiness. Set within him were the instruments of worship, tabrets and pipes and within his mind was the desire to lead the angelic host in the most beautifully composed and deeply reverential worship of which they were capable.

As Lucifer raised his hands a gentle hush descended and his music and voice was heard as he began to worship and adore the Lord of the universe. The angelic throng, their combined depth of sincerity and completeness transcending their individual capacities, joined Lucifer. They were united in a holistic act of worship that elevated them to that place of rapture, that is only possible to attain when all is being given to the One who is "All in All". Lucifer heard the most beautiful sounds in the universe as the voices of the other angels combined with his, to produce a mosaic of harmonious perfection that worshipped and honoured the Lord of All. He looked out and around at the angelic host and felt the absolute totality of the love and exaltation that was flowing to the Father. As he stood in front of Majesty's throne experiencing the magnitude and depth of the worship, Lucifer was struck, almost physically, by its power.

For aeons past, a thought had been growing within him. It had started as an abstract and remote suggestion upon which he had pondered lightly. He had caressed it and allowed himself the luxury of imagining it was his, until it had become a definite goal and he realised how much he wanted to be worshipped. The desire took on a motivation and life of its own. It had expanded, deepened and grown until it exploded into an addictive passion that consumed his thoughts. Now he wanted that worship for himself more than anything else. He revelled in the elevation to deity and Godhead, that his out of control desire and imagination superimposed upon him. He had to have the reality of his imaginings and was now ready to pay any price for it.

In the past he had often sought to justify this corrupt desire and now closing his eyes to shut out the Father's presence he reasoned with himself. "Am I not the anointed cherub, am I not gifted with knowledge? Do I not walk in Eden, the garden of God, and upon the holy mountain? Does not my beauty surpass all others and am I not perfect in all my ways, am I not therefore worthy to receive this worship, is it not mine to take to myself?" As he answered "Yes" to each of these questions, Lucifer's self-deception became absolute as he set himself above the Lord of the Universe and took the worship to himself. He was instantly aware of its power within his spirit as it elevated him and gave him the ultimate status. He breathed a deep sigh of satisfaction at having received, that which he had desired for so long, reveling in the false majesty of his own deception.

The Holy Spirit felt the change in emphasis and knew precisely what had happened. The Spirit's heart was grieved as he looked upon the corruptness of Lucifer's condition and saw the Son of the Morning fallen from grace. He was further saddened as events continued to unfold.

The worshipping angels, discerning the spiritual change, knew that Lucifer was taking their worship for himself. They began to exercise their free wills as they endeavoured to decide to whom they would direct their worship, to Lucifer or the Father. For some, Lucifer's magnetic attraction proved too strong and they quickly surrendered to the strength of his will. Others resisted initially, continuing to worship the Father until Lucifer's hypnotic power could be withstood no longer.

Their surrender to him came with some reluctance but their capture was ensured. For quite a large group, their determination to resist, was not overcome until they realised that this usurper's throne was being set above the throne of God. That their allegiance to him might mean that they could share in his power and glory. The infection that entered their hearts produced a cancer of ambition that fueled a demonic furnace of instant explosive corruption. Suddenly, they knew that no matter what it cost them, they wanted for themselves a portion of what they believed Lucifer was in the process of achieving and they chose to worship Lucifer, rather than the Father.

The final group of angels that fell that day, did so out of misplaced loyalty to Lucifer and they reasoned, "Was he not their leader? Had he not always honoured the Lord, led their worship and served Him with devotion. Had they not always been subject to him and obeyed his commands? Was his rank and position not firmly established and recognized? Had the Father not given him immense beauty and wealth and did that not signify the Lord of Glory's acceptance and approval of him? Of course it did! Were not devotion, obedience and loyalty Kingdom principles, that provided the structure and fabric of an angel's life?"

Lucifer, now holding the centre stage of their attention, became their focus. Their loyalty cemented them to him and sealed their fate.

Amongst the rest of the angels, solidarity emerged as they began to comprehend the full horror of what was happening. The great warrior angel, Michael, Captain of the Host, was incredulous when he realised the magnitude of Lucifer's pride, ambition and arrogance. He had before him and under his command, many armies of highly trained warrior angels that would look to him for leadership and direction.

The worship now died away and was replaced by an

awkward silence. Lucifer opened his eyes as anger at being denied the worship he craved welled up inside him. He roared blasphemous obscenities at the top of his voice, as he rose to his full height his face contorted into a mask of hatred. This cataclysmic change in his personality coincided with a physical manifestation within the angelic assembly.

Throughout this massive congregation, haloes of crystal light were being extinguished as angels came under Lucifer's domination. As angel after angel decided to give their loyalty to Lucifer, corruption came upon them and they fell from grace, lost their holiness and their haloes of crystal light. They were engulfed in spiritual and physical darkness. Throughout the angelic assembly pinpoints and patches of blackness were appearing.

As the contamination spread whole areas of darkness became evident as holiness and righteousness were given over to corruption and evil. The darkness continued to spread until it encompassed a third of the angelic host.

Lucifer saw what was happening and was filled with pride. His ego inflated as he realised the size of the angelic following that was his. Not only were numbers of seraphim and cherubim involved, but also of every other category and type of angel; some had exercised their free will and given their loyalty to him. Perhaps nowhere was this to have a more immediate effect than amongst the warrior angels of Michael's armies. It soon became apparent that significant numbers were now bowing the knee to Lucifer and large areas of blackness indicated where whole armies had given their allegiance to him.

Michael looked about and was aware of what was taking

place. As he peered into the dark area nearest to him, he could see the horrendous transformations that were occurring in the appearance and nature of the angels that had given themselves to Lucifer. No longer were they entitled to the angelic form that is reserved for God's messengers and servants. Their halos had gone, so too their white garments and silky wings. The change in their appearance happened simultaneously with their decision to worship Lucifer, for in that moment their thinking aligned to satanic values. The bodies they now inhabited, reflected the rebellious condition of their hearts and the corruption of their minds.

The darkness that surrounded them could not hide what was happening, for what had been light and beauty was now black and ugly. Many had become reptilian in appearance and Michael could clearly discern the yellow fangs that protruded from their mouths dripping green slime.

As Michael moved his gaze within the darkness, large yellow eyes filled with hatred and viciousness looked back at him. The noises that came from these demonic creatures were mostly unintelligible to him and made his skin crawl. They were communicating in what sounded like blasphemous grunts and curses, pitched low in their throats as they swayed and shuffled in irritation and anger. They emitted the smell of sulphur that came strongly to his nostrils.

Knowing the time had come for action, Michael drew his sword and rose bodily above everyone else. He shouted the order that would bring the commanders of his armies to his side. From throughout this massive assembly streaks of light appeared shooting upwards towards him. The generals of the armies of the Lord of Hosts now gathered in front of Michael, their Commanding Officer. Each of them was a magnificent angel, holy and righteous, and totally committed to the service of the Lord. They represented the best that Heaven had. As Michael ran through their names in his mind, he was grieved to realise that two were missing, for even the best can succumb to temptation. He spoke to them, "This day sin has entered this most holy place and many of our brethren have left our ranks having chosen to worship Lucifer rather than the Lord of Life. This most serious transgression has resulted in their spiritual and bodily corruption, the evidence of which you will have seen. We must be ready to do battle for they now stand against us and all that Heaven represents. Go now and lead your warriors in the service of the Lord and His kingdom and may His blessing be upon you."

As he spoke Michael was aware of movement beneath him and as he returned to the main gathering he could see that while he had been away Lucifer had been active. Now, instead of pinpoints and portions of darkness dispersed throughout the assembly, there was one large black area signifying that all the fallen angels had come together. He could see Lucifer standing in their midst speaking to them and heard him saying in brutal tones, "You are mine and I demand absolute obedience. You will do exactly as I say or my vengeance will be upon you and I will destroy you! I am the Mighty One and you will worship none other but me. There is no God above me. My throne is absolute and my authority beyond question. Do you understand?"

As Lucifer spoke his countenance began to change and

darkness came over him. His voice became a harsh growl and black emissions puffed from his nostrils. His form became that of a dragon, red in colour, scaly, ugly and horrible. The stench that came from him was that of sulphur and rotting flesh. His agitation, impatience and anger was apparent from the irritated movements he made as he shifted his weight from foot to foot and emitted guttural grunts as he spoke, "This is my kingdom and I share it with no one! I am the Lord of the universe and my throne is set above all others. You will worship me alone. I am the destroyer of all that displeases me and my kingdom is a kingdom of deception and destruction."

The demonic had taken hold and a total transformation was occurring as Lucifer spoke. He had become the "Great Red Dragon" and the fallen angels that now stood with him had become demons. Lucifer had become Satan.

C 3

JUDGEMENT

There was absolute silence and stillness in Heaven and a deep sadness pervaded the Kingdom. For the first time in eternity, praise was not being heard and the wings of angels were stilled.

The Holy Spirit brooded as He considered the magnitude of recent events knowing that a fundamental change had occurred and that there could be no going back to the joy and innocence of the past.

The seriousness of the situation affected everyone and many heavenly beings were thinking deeply of what the future might hold. All were ashamed of the actions of the angels who had rebelled and fallen from grace. Many, were grieving for friends and loved ones who had given their allegiance to Lucifer or who had been lost in the battle.

Members of the Angelic Host had always known that when the Father had designed, created and formed them, He had given the precious gift of free will. They knew they were not automatons, programmed to behave in a particular way, but thinking beings with the ability to make choices and the freedom to decide their own course of action. The Holy Spirit desired to help them in the decision-making processes but His honouring of their free will, prevented any suggestion of Him imposing His will on them. He came into their lives only by invitation.

In a far corner of Heaven, Satan and his demons were held imprisoned by chains and darkness. Around them stood a guard of mighty warrior angels, their wings unfurled and their swords drawn. The demons were contained; there would be no escaping the consequences of their rebellious actions and corrupt hearts. They had made the decision to align with Lucifer and now must pay the price for that choice.

The angels on guard duty were not enjoying their role. The demons were showing their true colours and their fallen natures could be both seen and heard. The language they used was disgusting and the angels within earshot were appalled at the filth coming from their mouths. It was as though the holiness of the angels was being challenged by the corruption, that was so much part of each demonic being. They shuffled in irritation and impatience, moving their feet as far as their chains would allow whilst cursing and blaspheming, voicing the most hideous thoughts, which poured from their mouths as foul words and sounds. The fallen spirit always contains some of the characteristics of Satan himself and the depraved and vicious qualities now being displayed, came straight from the portals and depths of Hell.

At every opportunity, and whenever they were within striking distance of each other, their teeth, claws and tails were used to the most damaging effect. They bit, clawed and thrashed and the screams of the injured could be clearly heard over the punishing shouts and roars of those inflicting the damage. Where attacks had resulted in injury, blood was flowing freely. Cuts and gashes dripped green and black slime, forming pools and puddles on the ground. Limbs that had been severed lay where they had fallen.

The angels guarding their prisoners were in no way prepared for this antagonistic and abusive behaviour and had to quickly adjust to the malicious ways in which the demons related to each other. They soon realised that what they were seeing was so completely different from the care and consideration they showed to one another. If it had not been for their warrior hearts they could not have coped with this vicious culture. At first they had been quite stunned by the demons' behaviour but were learning fast the ways of those who had alienated themselves from the influence of the Holy Spirit and the love of God, the Father.

The defeated demon army was all together in one place and they affected the atmosphere around them by giving off a coldness that was numbing. It radiated from them, lowering the temperature and chilling the angels guarding them, causing them to fold their wings around their bodies in an effort to keep warm.

The angels had no experience of fallenness and were ignorant of the effects it produced; consequently struggling with a number of issues they were now experiencing. Not only was the steep drop in temperature a problem but they also had to deal with the awful smell of the demons that seemed to come from every part of them. Their breath was appalling and their bodies gave off the most intense odours, that caused the angels to gag and retch. It wafted to them as a mixture of sulphur, decaying vegetation and rotting flesh. They used the tips of their wings to fan the area in front of their faces to gain some relief. The angels had until now known only the fragrance of the Holy Spirit, that is reminiscent of spring flowers blended to aromatic perfection. This was in total contrast to the incredible stench to which they were now subjected.

This situation was soon to change. The arrival of Gabriel, the head of the Messenger Corp saw to that. The golden sheen of his silken wings reflected the light of his glowing countenance as he sought out Loyola, the Commander of the Guard and spoke with him, "Greetings my friend. I bring you the Father's wishes, for He desires that the judgment of Satan and his followers take place in the area before his throne. I am also instructed to say that there is to be a procession of your prisoners from here and Majesty suggests a double line of warriors to secure the route."

Gabriel then became aware of the coldness coming from the demons and the strength of the smell they were emitting. He folded his wings around him and fanned his face as the other angels were doing. He went on, "No doubt you will be glad when this sorry business is over and life has returned to normal."

Loyola pulled a face to acknowledge his friends discomfort at the smell and said, "I'm not sure just how hard it will be to move this lot en masse. They're a surly bunch at the best of times, never seeming to stop fighting amongst themselves and are giving us all kinds of strife. Have you seen the damage they've done to each other, it's hard to believe they are on the same side? With friends like these fellows you certainly don't need enemies!"

Gabriel grinned and replied, "I really don't envy your task, and wish you well for tomorrow. May the Lord's blessing be with you." He left in a blaze of crystal light whilst leaving a trail of sparkling diamond points behind him.

The following morning as preparation was made for the demons to be moved they soon realised what was afoot and did all they could to be difficult and objectionable. They taunted their captors with ribald comments aimed at undermining their authority and self-confidence. They refused to line up and move off in an orderly manner. They squabbled and fought at every opportunity and sorely tried the patience of the angels guarding them.

After several false starts Loyola called his Section Commanders together and spoke to them firmly, "If we are to successfully complete our task and have these reprobates before the Father, then our attitude must change! I want to see you using far more authority. You and the angels under your command are to stand firm against the will of the demons. You must take charge of the situation and not allow the demons to have control. You are members of the Kingdom of Heaven and as such have been given authority over them. I want to see that authority being used. You have hearts of faith and are well armed both spiritually and physically. The demons are spirit beings and are subject to us 'in the spirit'."

Loyola continued, "You must be prepared to use your authority and the spiritual weapons at your disposal. Your word of command has great power, use it to overcome the forces of darkness and so achieve the purposes of the Father's Kingdom. I require you to speak to your subordinates as I have spoken to you. Now return to your positions and exercise the power you have at your disposal. Go with the Lord's blessing."

The Section Commanders grew in stature as Loyola spoke. Their heads came up and they stood tall as they were reminded of their authority as members of the Kingdom of God. They returned to their commands with a new resolve, and they were to be heard speaking strongly and resolutely to those under them.

The situation changed markedly as the mouths of the demons were stopped by angelic command. Orders were now issued with a newfound authority and complied with instantly. The angels were soon firmly in control and the procession quickly assembled, ready to move off towards the coming judgement.

At the front of the procession were the remaining dragons, their fires extinguished, their spirits depressed by defeat. After them the scorpions, some showing the scars of battle, with the ends of their tails missing. All of them carrying the visual evidence of their defeat, with their tails no longer being held over their heads in the attack position but dragging behind them. Gone was the proud arrogance that they had shown on entering the battle. Many of the giant spiders had legs missing and moved with an uneven gait.

Satan was considered too dangerous for release and remained confined within the net that held him, and now his disgrace was made complete by the arrival of the elite Special Forces Regiment. Its members were angels of such size and stature, as to be revered by all who came into contact with them. They were five hundred strong and their commission was to ensure that Satan did not escape. They arrived in arrow point formation, flying very low at almost supersonic speed, a streak of scarlet light emblazoned across the horizon. As they approached the spot where Satan was contained they pulled up into a vertical climb and executed a stunning bomb-burst maneuver, which as they broke formation and descended, positioned them precisely around Satan and the net in which he was contained.

The two mighty angels in charge of the net now moved forcefully in opposite directions, whilst pulling strongly on the rope that would open the mouth of the net and release Satan from his confinement. The whole operation appeared as a beautifully choreographed movement, for at the same moment as Satan was released the Special Forces' angels descended around him in a 'flying box' formation.

One hundred of them formed a canopy fifty feet above him whilst the rest formed the four sides of the box. Each angel arrived with sword drawn, revealing the silver handles and golden cutting edges on the broad bladed swords they carried, this being the mark of their Unit's élan. Every sword was held so that its tip was pointed inwards towards Satan, making it very clear that they were resolved to deal swiftly and firmly with any attempt to escape.

Contained by the angels of the Special Forces Regiment a defeated and morose Satan could do nothing but accept the humiliation. The procession was now able to move off and made its way between the double line of angels guarding the route. At its fore was the 'flying box' with Satan shambling along dispirited, his great tail dragging behind him.

As the procession approached the area in which God's throne was situated, the demons became very aware of His presence. The atmosphere through which they were moving changed and contained more and more of Majesty's radiant holiness. The corruption and evil contained within their own psyches stood in stark contrast to the Father's righteousness. They felt as though they were moving through a substance that was becoming progressively denser and repulsive to them the further on they went.

To move deeper into His presence they had to overcome their natural desire to be anywhere but where they were. Their spirits resisted the Holy Presence, and had it not been for the angels and the sharpness of their swords in close proximity to them, they would not have continued.

Finally, this enormous procession arrived at its destination and assembled before the throne of God! The Father's presence was now so manifest, as to be both physically and spiritually tangible and permeated the atmosphere in which the demons stood and the very air they breathed.

The discomfort of the demons was made even more intense by the sound of angelic voices softly offering worship to the Father. This was their first encounter with this phenomenon since their downfall.

Now the very fabric of their existence cried out in protest at being in close proximity to a holy God. Their spiritual corruption stood in stark contrast to the holiness of the Father and the worshipping angels. The clash of kingdoms was extreme and they wanted to be anywhere but where they were.

Standing on either side of God's throne were six angels, each with a golden band around their waist and a silver trumpet in their right hand. Their hair was silken to their shoulders and they were dressed in white robes that reached to their ankles. Upon their feet were golden shoes, set with precious stones that sparkled and shone. In a synchronized movement they raised the trumpets to their lips and blew a mighty stanza that heralded the Father's presence. As the sound died away an enormous angel, magnificent in splendour and who was robed in scarlet, raised a scroll that he held at arm's length. After unrolling it he read the following, "This Holy and royal court is convened by order of the Lord of Heaven. The judgements that will be given concern the fallen angel Lucifer and the angels that followed him in rebellion.

It is the Father's judgement that you, Lucifer, did desire to take to yourself the worship that is rightfully His and to set your throne above His. You were the Bearer of the Light, and you were trusted with the light. Built within you, and given to you from the time you were created was the means of offering and leading worship, which is the ministry of the Light. You, Lucifer, were master of all and in your righteousness you lived and walked in perfection, but in one moment all that changed.

You, Lucifer, began to yearn in your heart more for the Light than for your Lord. In that instant the defects in your character were exposed. In that moment of frailty you took to yourself personal sovereignty and said in your heart that you were above the God that created you and gave you life.

Lucifer, you know the Father desires rightness of character more than anything, for it is out of character that understanding and actions come. It is out of strength of character that true worship of mind and heart flows from an individual to the Father. The Father will only receive and take to himself worship that is freely and wholeheartedly given. For worship to be valued by Him, it must come from a sacrificial outpouring of love and adoration from deep within the giver. You, Lucifer, stopped giving your worship freely and desired to receive the worship of others. Even more than that, you influenced other members of the angelic host to direct their worship to you. In that way you corrupted them and sowed the seeds of their downfall.

The Father decrees there is no longer a place in Heaven for you and the angels that worshipped you, and you are all to be removed from Heaven and cast down to the Earth."

On hearing this, Satan straightened his back and planted his feet firmly where he stood, his great tail straightened and he lifted his head to speak. A slyness of countenance came over him and out of a deception borne of his corruption, he spoke from his heart in a most pleading and pathetic manner, "This judgement is most unjust! In doing what I did I was only complying with the wishes of the angelic host who prompted me. They put me up to it, they wanted me to rule Heaven. I was manipulated by them and am not to blame for what has happened, they are!"

He went on pathetically, "Nobody knows the pressure I have been under from them. They kept asking and begging me to take over the rule of the Kingdom and now I am to be punished and cast away from the God I love and have served faithfully for so long." He turned his head and a crocodile tear came from the corner of his eye and ran down his scaly nose. He went on, "Can you not see, O Lord of Heaven, that I am your most faithful and devoted servant and want nothing more than to worship and serve you. Let me remain here with you, for it is these who are the originators of this transgression and it is they who deserve to be severely punished, not I. Cast them out and I will remain and serve you." As he spoke Satan pointed with his tail at the assembled fallen angels to make it quite clear whom he was accusing.

The massive and glorious angel holding the scroll turned to face Satan and looked full into his eyes, the compassion that was there when he first started to speak, was now replaced by resolute contempt. His face had hardened and it was obvious that he viewed this transgressor as an enemy and wanted only for their interaction to be at an end. He spoke, "There was a time, Satan, when you were my superior and I respected and revered you. You were an example to us all and we aspired to be like you, but since iniquity has been found in you, the changes that have taken place in your allegiance, values, morals and perspective have left you unfit for the service of the Lord. It is not possible for you to remain in this holy place for your heart desires only to steal, kill and destroy. The contamination of your mind and spirit is absolute and your body, so dramatically changed, is visual evidence of the transformation that has taken place throughout your being. You are responsible for your own degradation and nobody else is to blame!

Not only have you brought yourself to a place of decadence, decay and disgust, but you have also used your power and influence to bring down many of your colleagues and subordinates, who held you in high esteem. You were Lucifer, the 'Bearer of the Light,' but you have, of your own volition, become an anathema to this holy place and to the remaining angelic host.

You had so much, and you misused all which had been bestowed upon you. Now you must accept the consequences of your deeds and spend eternity in spiritual darkness, separated from the Father and the love and joy of His presence. You have heard the Father's judgement and are to be cast down to the Earth and I trust that this is the last we shall see of you!"

With these words the angel rolled up the scroll with a crispness that clearly said judgement had been given and the audience was at an end.

Satan opened his mouth to protest but before the words could be uttered, he felt the presence of the Living God envelop him, not just him but his demon hordes as well. It was an all embracing encounter, that they experienced as every part of their vile beings was engulfed, surrounded, impacted and penetrated by the power of the Holy Spirit. Each demon began to squirm and to feel physically sick, as the Holiness of the Lord's presence clashed with their corrupt spirits and fallen natures. They involuntarily expelled air from their lungs and made a loud groaning noise that expressed the revulsion they felt, as the absolute power of Sovereign Righteousness took hold of them and bodily lifted them en masse.

For an instant time and space were suspended. They

were thrust at the speed of light out of the portals of Heaven and into an inky blackness that produced confusion and disorientation in each of them. It was as if a tunnel of darkness was controlling their direction as they sped towards their new destination.

Groan Earth, for the Devil and his angels are cast down to you!

C4

CAST DOWN

The divine spark of life had been imparted with plants and animals being born, living and dying in the time-span allotted to them. The Earth teemed with life and life was good.

Trees and vegetation displayed a profusion of shapes and sizes as they reached upward towards the sun, stretching, growing and basking in its warmth, delighting in its power to impart growth and to be the catalyst for life. The hues and textures of a multiplicity of plants favoured many shades of green with speckled sunlight dancing on their leaves. Vast arrays of brightly coloured flowers shared the ground with grasses of many textures. Flowers held their heads high to receive more of the life giving sunlight as it radiated to them. Rolling hills and craggy peaks completed the vista with colours ranging from the soft browns of the soil to the grey and black of the rocks, hills and mountains.

The planet Earth turned on its axis and rotated in space, following its predetermined orbit around the sun. Time passed and as the sun continued to warm the planet's surface, moisture rose from its pools, ponds, rivers, lakes and seas. A profusion of clouds formed in the warm moist air and became a partial canopy beneath which a vast array of creatures lived their lives on the Earth's surface, in its seas, within its soil and in the sky overhead. High above in the powder blue sky, puffy white and grey clouds rolled and swayed, pushed along by unseen winds, ever moving, stretching, reaching and changing.

Over this landscape the presence of God moved. He touched and caressed His creation and was pleased with it. The colours and textures satisfied His eyes and the diverse beauty of shape and function struck a deep chord that made His heart sing with joy.

Yet, somehow there was something lacking and it was a while before He realised just what it was. He could speak to creation, in fact He had spoken it into being, but it was a one-way conversation; He longed for a two-way dialogue. He could relate to creation but creation could not relate meaningfully to Him.

The Father looked around as He pondered this problem. The hills, lakes, trees and plants were beautiful but they lacked the ability to communicate. They could not communicate with Him on a personal level and that was what He was missing. They had form and function but could not think, reason or speak. What He had created so far did not have the capacity to satisfy His longing for relationship.

He decided what He would do. It was risky He knew to move from inanimate creation to created beings who had the ability to think and speak. Particularly so, if their thoughts were in no way controlled by Him but He reasoned, to gain what He desired was worth taking the risk.

The Lord Creator, desiring to have a truly meaningful relationship with mankind, men and women made in His own image. He gave them a spirit with which to relate to Him. A body to move around in the midst of His creation, a mind enabling them to think; emotions with which to feel and a will with which to exercise freedom of choice. He befriended mankind and delighted in their company, talking with them and walking with them amongst the plants and flowers in the cool of the evening, enjoying conversation, fellowship and unity with them.

The relationship between the Creator and humankind blossomed and grew. A deep respect was established between them with the sovereign Lord honouring the independence that He had given and human beings worshipping and holding in awe, the God who graced their lives with His presence and friendship. Both creator God and created beings looked forward to their regular daily meetings with eagerness, born of true affection and a deepening desire to commune in an unsurpassed depth of relationship.

Into this utopia came a massively corruptive influence as Satan and his fallen angels touched down on the Earth. Silently, oh so silently they came and with great stealth secreted themselves in a hidden place. These pinnacles of satanic degradation and filth hid themselves away so that they would be maximally effective in their diabolically corrosive and destructive intentions.

Satan was well aware of the beautiful relationship that had developed between God and mankind. He and his spies had hidden and watched the interaction, hating every moment of their closeness and harmony. His teeth ground in anger and frustration when men and women bowed the knee and worshipped the Living God. He had seen their hands raised in adoration and praise and had heard the sweetness of their voices in song and prayer. He fumed and cursed at the giving of devotion to anyone other than himself. The absolute corruption of his heart and mind left no possibility for anything other than the fulfilment of his own, despicably self-centered ambition and heinous desires. These were driven by the absolute imperative he felt to be the God who was worshipped by all creation. His mind worked overtime as he schemed and planned the strategies that would ensure his ambitions would be achieved.

The first action that Satan took was to call an Orders Group to be attended by all Generals and Battalion Commanders. They assembled before him, their black oiled armour creaking lightly at the joints, their swords scabbarded and their heads bare of helmets. Each one knelt and worshipped him, knowing that if they did not their life would end immediately. The atmosphere was tense with fear, which had become the hallmark of Satan's authority. He received their oblations as his right and ordering them into a tight group before him spoke in a measured tone, his gravelly voice spitting out the words that would lead to degradation, destruction and death for so many.

He began, "Dominion over the Earth has been given to those miserable creatures known as 'mankind' but I will rule and reign in their lives, for they will surrender their sovereignty and freedom to me! The Earth and all within it will be mine and I will be the sovereign Lord of the Earth!

Each one of you and all those that you command, will without question, obey my orders precisely and do exactly as I say, for I will have absolute obedience from you all. I have a slow and painful death waiting any who question my authority or try my patience."

As Satan spoke he stamped his right foreleg on the ground to emphasize his main points, and his great scaly tail wove constantly from left to right and back again, a slow rhythmic movement behind him creating a visual effect that signaled the shortness of his temper and the power of his being. His nostrils dilated as orange flame singed the air in front of him causing the front rank to lean back sharply, as they felt the intense heat of his potential wrath. They all clearly understood whom they served!

He continued, "We all have much work to do if my domination over the world is to be absolute, and I assure you, it will be! The reconnaissance that has been carried out so far, indicates a strong relationship between mankind and Him and that is the first thing that needs our attention. It's fortuitous that when humans were designed He was stupid enough to give them free will and it is this mistake that we will use to very good effect. We will see who they end up serving and worshipping."

As Satan finished speaking he broke into cackling laughter that was both mirthless, hollow and hideous. It started way down in his chest and erupted through his cavernous mouth where it gave vocal expression to the contempt that he felt for the fallen angels. They were his subordinates but more especially, the Lord Creator God whom he was determined to usurp. The demons, seeking to curry favour, started to mimic this satanic mirth and taking their lead from their Master cackled along with him, an inverted merriment that was neither happy nor joyous and which had contempt at its root.

Suddenly, Satan's demeanor changed as his laughter slowed and quieted until it petered out completely. Deep thought furrowed his scaly brow as he began to think in a strategic way. He lowered his head and pondered thoughtfully before he spoke again to his minions. At the same instant a transformation took place in his bodily appearance.

Magically his substance mutated as his outer appearance vibrated and shook and for a split second became translucent. Spontaneously the Great Dragon's form both dissolved and was reconstituted in a totally different format. He had changed in both colour and texture. His appearance was no longer that of an enormous dragon, but had instantly mutated in both form and substance. Horns and cloven hoofs appeared and goat hair covered his body. He was transformed before their eyes as he transmogrified into a goat-like appearance. In just a second or two the process was complete and now the evil that emanated from him, seemed to have been amplified many times as the darkness of his countenance struck a deeper and more terrifying fear into the hearts and minds of his subordinate demons.

Standing on his hind legs, Satan towered over them and waited briefly whilst they recovered from their shock and assimilated his changed appearance. He gloated inwardly at the reaction of deepened fear that was so apparent. Their wide bulging eyes and the involuntary gasp they had all simultaneously emitted, confirmed that he had timed the surprise of his transformation correctly and had achieved maximum impact!

"Shut up and listen!" He growled, pausing until they had recovered their composure. "We must plan carefully," he said, "the relationship between the Father…" as he spoke the word 'Father', he spat green bile onto the ground before him, "and the humans, must be broken. I have decided that this is our first and foremost priority."

As Satan finished speaking a voice spoke from in front of the assembled commanders. It was Znelka, the Head of the Chiefs of Staff, standing tall and erect with the light glinting on the black metal inserts of his armour. The green scales on his face were scarred as evidence of his service as a warrior. Taking his helmet from under his left arm, he held it above his bony rounded cranium and slowly lowered it into position until it covered his head and face and sat lightly on his shoulders. He turned slightly to his right until he faced Satan, his Commander in Chief, and as he did so his gauntleted right hand reached across his body to the hilt of his sword and grasped its ebony and gold hand-piece. With a slow, deliberate and purposeful movement he drew the sword from its jewel-encrusted scabbard. As he did so the blackness of the wickedly curved blade contrasted with the sword's cutting edge that glowed crimson, designating Znelka's high rank.

As he began to speak he brought his sword from the ceremonial carry position, vertically in front of his body, and lowered its tip in salute till it almost touched the ground directly in front of Satan and just a sword's length from him. His voice came strong and clear, "Lord Satan, I salute you! You are our god and we worship and honour you. We give you our obedience, our commitment to your purposes and if necessary, we will give you our lives. Use us, as you will. We are yours."

His voice rose in volume until it became a great crescendo, an ear splitting cry of, *"We are yours! We are yours! We are yours! We are yours!"*

Znelka's actions and speech had an electrifying effect on the other senior demon officers, who rose to their feet as one, and each drawing his sword brandished it above his head, shouting, *"We are yours! We are yours! We are yours!"*

In the fervour of excitement, and commonality of purpose, the commanders of Satan's demon army, committed themselves to breaking the relationship between God the Father and human beings.

Satan looked on, pleased with their demonstration of loyalty. Even more satisfied and delighted with the fear he was sure he had imparted to their psyches and the increased control he was now certain he exercised over them. He raised his cloven forelegs and signaled for silence. The passions that had been aroused took a moment or two to subside and then he motioned for them to gather closely in front of him. He began to speak, "I have made a careful study of the creatures we know as humans, for I was there when they were given dominion over this planet and over every plant and animal. I have deduced that they will be extremely vulnerable to us if we employ certain strategic principles.

The first thing I want you all to clearly understand, is that the battle is for their minds. We are going to control their thoughts and that means we are going to put into their minds the fallen values, ethics, standards and behaviours that we have and need them to have. We will infect their minds with lust, sexual perversions and pornography. We will implant fake religions and the worship of false gods. We will break their relationships and cause social disharmony and strife within their homes. We will assault their integrity and attack their morality until dishonesty and aggression are normal to them.

Their countries will go to war with each other and there will be bloodshed and death across their lands. I will have control over what they think and will influence every aspect of their lives. Then I will be able to control everything they do and the quality of every relationship they have, especially their relationship with Him!

I intend to change their values, corrupt their standards and undermine their ethics, so that their behaviour becomes an abomination to Him. They will be brought down to where we are, and I will be their ruler and have dominion over them. Not just them but also their children and their children's children. They will all be part of my kingdom. I will be their god and they will obey me and worship me for all eternity."

As he spoke, Satan was imagining what it would be like to receive the worship of humans, both now and far into the future. His eyes glassed over as he anticipated the bliss that was to be his and filled him with ecstasy. In his mind he was already experiencing the delights to come. He closed his eyes and swayed a little unsteadily from side to side, allowing himself this pinnacle of status and pleasure, if only in his imagination.

The senior demons looking on decided that discretion was the better part of valour and although they would have liked to take advantage of their leader's ecstatic state, had a clear understanding of the violence that he could so swiftly and easily unleash against them.

It was Znelka who was first to begin to worship. He raised his hands and began to sing an offering to his Lord Satan. The sound that came from him was vilely disharmonious and as the other demons joined in the cacophony, what they produced was almost beyond comprehension in its fragmentation and discordance.

Slowly Satan opened his eyes and seeing the scene before him, was aware of the demons' endeavours to elevate him to the highest place; he was pleased with their worship and took it to himself. As he did so he could feel his power increasing and he willed for more and more of the same. It was a long time before the worship came to an end and Satan's strategic planning meeting was able to continue. When it did, it was very apparent that there was much ground to cover and many schemes to develop.

The meeting reconvened in a clearing deep in a forest, where the upward slope of the ground and the curve of the area clear of the giant trees formed a natural amphitheater. The trees towered above them as the demon commanders prepared for their next briefing. They had unbuckled their swords and relaxed as best they could by sitting on their shields. It was twilight and as the light continued to fade and the breeze ebbed away, the stillness of the night was under-girded by the fear and tension that was in the black trembling heart of each demon. An unholy atmosphere settled on the place.

Satan, in his form of the great hairy goat, stood on his hind legs before them and instantly took control of the proceedings by insisting on absolute silence. His yellow eyes, with their deep black oblong pupils, which had an almost hypnotic power, commanded their attention and made it clear that he was there to speak and they were there to listen.

As the moon rose, so the pale light it emitted fell on the clearing and basked everything in its yellow presence. Satan stood with the soft light directly behind him, which gave the effect of him being surrounded by an almost golden halo. His enormous goat-like form clearly silhouetted against the yellow disc of the moon, which sat low on the horizon just above the tree line. His outline was clear but the details of his form were masked whilst giving the impression that his voice was coming from outside of himself, almost as though it were a detached entity.

The shape of the amphitheater projected his words forward where they bounced off the upward sloping bank and were deflected to the sides where the demons sat. To them his voice sounded amplified and with the hint of an echo, as though coming from all directions at once.

Satan paused and waited until he was certain that all eyes were firmly fixed upon him and every movement had ceased and every rustle stilled. Then, drawing himself up to his full stature he began to speak, softly at first, but with each word his voice gained in intensity and volume, "In the past our role as angels was to bring help and blessing but we have changed and our motivations, intentions and functions have changed. We will now bring depravity, disease, desecration, destruction and death to all those we can influence and we will affect the whole of mankind. Every part of creation will be subject to us!"

Now at maximum volume the bass tones of his voice reverberated across the clearing and waving and gesticulating with his forelegs and with dark green spittle, showering from his mouth and falling on those directly in front of him, he continued, *"Human beings are weak and will be like clay in my hands. I will mold them and shape them and bring them down. They will obey me and I will be their Lord and their God. They will worship me!"*

The spittle that formed in his mouth pooled behind his green and black teeth and sprayed those closest to him as he spoke. The surplus saliva flowed out of the sides of his mouth and ran in rivulets down his chin and dripped spasmodically from the ends of his grey goatee beard. He continued to explain his plan, "The One who created them is a fool to have given them the free will that He gave us. He should have made them autonyms and programmed them to obey Him eternally. Now He will pay for His misplaced trust! We are going to seriously influence their thinking and give these humans a whole new values system. They are going to learn to desire the most corrupt moral and ethical values and they will engage in the most horrendous depravity. We are going to ensure they become apathetic towards Him and disobedient in every possible way. They will become rebellious, violent, independent, self- indulgent, gluttonous and corrupt."

As he spoke, so the pitch of his voice became lower and lower until it was a deep bass, coarse and gravely. He continued to address his army commanders, who without exception were listening with an intensity that was borne of the powerful demonic spirit that Satan emitted. It enveloped them and penetrated each one fixing their fallen spirits to his with a magnetism that bordered on the hypnotic. All of them felt his power and could not take their eyes from the oblong yellow pupils of his eyes. A trance-like state of mass aberration was developing as Satan's corrupting power locked the will of his subordinates into his evil desires.

He continued to speak, his voice and spiritual presence now over-powering any vestige of free will that may have remained, "We are going to create in the minds of these humans a very strong desire to worship and they will bow the knee to many figments of their imaginations. We are going to create and raise up a myriad of false gods for them to acknowledge, to sacrifice to, to do penance to and to offer their lives to. For it matters not to me whom they worship as long as it is not Him, for any worship not directed exclusively to Him will automatically come to me through these false gods."

Again he spat green bile onto the ground in front of them, but now he symbolically ground it into the earth with his hind legs in a visual display of contempt. Then he went on, "We are going to create a massive religious system that allows these humans all the choices they want and they will create their own gods. What they will not understand, is that whichever of the spiritual paths they choose they will be worshipping me." As he finished speaking, he momentarily closed his eyes and gave a deep sigh of satisfaction and remained transfixed by the anticipated power and pleasure he knew, would surely be his.

It was Znelka who broke the spell by speaking, his deep

bass voice resounding in the still night air, "Lord Satan, we recognise your right to receive worship and you will very soon be the ruler of this world, but what if some of the humans choose to worship 'Him,' rather than you my Lord?"

The effect of Znelka's words was electric. Satan's eyes snapped open and he spun round to face him. His anger ignited, he exploded in a torrent of vile abuse and animated hatred. He could barely speak for the rage within him knew no bounds, as he castigated his Commander in Chief, *"You dare to speak to me suggesting such a thing!"* His eyes had turned red and his face contorted into a mask of apocalyptic vengeance! He snarled his response, *"Imbecile, idiot, you cretinous dog. If that ever happens I will flay those responsible to within an inch of their life and feed them to the crocodiles. Your principle role, you maggot infested weasel, is to make absolutely sure that worship is not directed to Him."* Satan approached Znelka, who fell to his knees before him and drawing the sword of the demon nearest to him, thrust the tip of it into Znelka's throat and watched the black blood ooze and gurgle down the terrified demon's armour.

The assembled demons watched this display of brutality in horror. A new level of fear was injected into the heart of each of them. Having infected every demon present, the terror dynamic now took over and a deeper depth of satanic control established. Each demon felt terror permeate their being, producing a paralysing effect upon their minds. With breathing arrested and eyes wide and bulging they watched the ritual slaying of the most senior demon.

Satan smiled inwardly but outwardly ground his teeth in a display of anger and thrust the sword deeper into Znelka's throat. Znelka screamed for mercy that was not forthcoming and a fountain of black blood spurted skyward as the sword's blade severed the jugular vein. He fell forward and as he did so, Satan released the hilt of the sword from his grasp, allowing the blade to remain embedded in the throat of the dying demon. Znelka and the sword fell as one and lay in a growing pool of blood that continued to expand. He made gurgling noises from deep in his throat as his lungs filled with blood and struggled for air, his dying body jerked and twitched. The pool of blood continued to expand even after all movement had ceased and death had claimed him.

Satan turned to face the assembly and with his features contorted into a sneer, he spoke to the commanders of his demonic forces in a voice as hard as granite and totally devoid of emotion, "Be very sure indeed, that Znelka was truly fortunate that I permitted him to die quickly and cleanly. Make no mistake, the next one of you I execute will not receive the same privilege!"

The atmosphere was now pregnant with fear that threatened to burst forth and overwhelm the assembled demons. It hung over them like an icy covering and each one of them felt its deep penetration into the core of their being. It was paralysing in its magnitude, and yet had the ability to focus their minds on one thing and one thing only, they knew exactly where they stood with their Lord Satan!

The slaying of Znelka showed them very clearly that they were all absolutely expendable, that Satan did not value them and held them in no regard. They knew that he would deal with them even more brutally if they gave him the opportunity.

The realisation that they were nothing more than disposable nonentities, was now fully developed and they each knew they were disposable in the spiritual battles that lay ahead. The will to survive was strong in each one and every demon resolved there and then never to question anything Satan said and to be the most compliant and willing servant their Master could desire.

A chill settled on the night as Satan moved from beside the body of Znelka and unhurriedly took again his position in front of the assembly. His black passionless eyes held their attention almost hypnotically and he spoke with a deep sarcasm in his voice, "I see that I need a new Commander in Chief, whom I trust will not make the mistake that Znelka made. I now appoint you, Diablos, to replace him."

The demon to which Satan spoke lifted his hideous head, which looked like a distortion of a crocodile's snout covered with tufts of coconut hair. His large red eyes had ebony black triangular pupils and as he rose to his feet to accept his new commission, it was apparent that he stood head and shoulders above his compatriots. He moved forward in front of Satan and as he did so the assembled demons rose to their feet, placed their helmets on their heads, and lifted their shields to the carry position. In a savage way they appeared a professional force that was not to be challenged lightly.

In a guttural voice that rang with the power of command, Diablos brought those now under his authority to attention and gave the order, "General Salute, present arms." With incredible synchronisation the demons' right hands moved as one across their bodies, to grasp the hilts of their swords and with their left hands steadying their scabbards, swords were drawn and held vertically in front of their armoured breastplates. The precision of these military movements was impressive, and the sound of hundreds of swords being drawn simultaneously left a strong impression of cutting edge power.

Diablos paused, and then lowered the tip of his sword to the ground completing the salute. He spoke, "We salute you Lord Satan and worship and honour you, confirming our loyalty and allegiance to you. We are yours to command and our swords and our lives are yours."

Satan felt satisfaction deep within his chest but did not allow any visible sign of it to reach his features. He set his jaw and hardened his eyes before he spoke, "Your lives and the lives of those under your command are indeed mine, and I will expend them as I choose. Make no mistake about this. You may die cleanly in battle but get it wrong and I have a very special death waiting for you. Carry on Diablos." The hardness of his countenance was not lost on them.

Diablos raised his sword from the salute to the carry position; smartly about-turned and addressed his subordinate commanders as he gave the order, "Return swords." As a synchronised movement, each demon commander placed the tip of his sword into the opening at the top of their scabbard and ran the blade in before returning to the position of attention. Satan now addressed them again. His voice now full of congeniality and refined friendship, "Relax gentlemen, we will continue our briefing."

He now spoke softly and almost collaboratively to the assembly, "You have a unique opportunity to be part of my diabolical kingdom that will be established on the Earth. You will all serve my purposes in the corruption of the human race and so earn your right to everlasting damnation. Each one of you will command the forces under your control in specific theatres of operation and I require that you pay close attention to what I am about to say."

He paused and looked about him, his eyes resting momentarily on each of his senior officers. As he did so, it was as if each one was sure he felt the tip of a sword prick the skin of his neck and was aware of the malicious violence that was just beneath the surface, which could so easily and expediently be unleashed against him.

Satan now moved to centre stage and with the moon silhouetting him perfectly in its yellow glow, he began to unfold a plan so heinous as to cause the downfall, destruction and damnation of the human race.

Drawing himself up to his full height he spoke with an absolute authority that commanded attention and ensured that he would be obeyed without question. His words penetrated the minds of his senior demons like a sword penetrating the heart of a fallen enemy. He began, "Understand this; I say again, the battle is for their minds! If their thought-life is under our control it follows that their actions will be under our control. So our first task is to speak into their minds with corrupting thoughts that will be so delicious they will not want to resist them. They will willingly succumb to thinking and then acting in ways that are going to place them on the path that will become a downward spiral, all the way to the depths of Hell."

Satan stamped his left hind leg into the ground, moving

it in a twisting motion to indicate the grinding into the dust of the human race and the contempt he felt for those soon to be tempted to their destruction. The listening demons understood the savage potential of what they were being told and the power that was to be theirs. They warmed with satisfaction to the concept, with deep-throated grunts and chuckles. To show their willing collaboration they began a light rattling of their swords against their shields and Satan glowed with satisfaction.

C5
STRATEGIC PLAN

In the next few hours Satan outlined a plan that would ensure the corruption and fall of the human race. His first and greatest priority was to break the harmonious relationship that existed between the Father and humans. Then, to move them away from the righteousness in which they lived, into the sinfulness he desired and which would bring about their fall from grace and the serving of his evil purposes.

He outlined the concept of false gods and the worship of idols and presented to them a variety of ways in which this could be accomplished. He understood all too clearly that if faith in the living God could be undermined, there was every possibility it could be replaced with the desire to worship that which was seen, could be touched and held, rather than worshipping the true but unseen God. In this way the deep desire to worship, that Satan knew was part of every human being, would be channelled to him.

They warmed to the idea that as demons they could also be obeyed and worshipped, but were cautioned to remember that any deference or worship they did receive was to be expediently channelled downwards to their Lord and Master, Satan.

He talked expansively concerning mind control and how to implant corrosive ideas and manipulate a humans' thought-life. Also, once a chink appeared in a person's character and they were accepting of a sinful thought or action, how to fill that opening and widen it with gratuitous desires that were base and self-destructive. He instructed, concerning the way to progressively bring down a human being by starting small and building a corrupt character piece by piece.

Another major concept was the encouragement of ambitious men and women who craved power; how that power could be made available to them. Satan explained how those people would then be used as major satanic agents to bring poverty, starvation, destruction and death to the masses. Satan set in their minds the truth of the words, "Power corrupts and absolute power corrupts absolutely." He outlined his plan to raise up many such despots that would do his bidding whilst they ruled groups, communities, tribes, cities and nations.

Until their Lord Satan explained it to them, they had not realised that they could live and abide within a human being. This revelation changed the situation for them considerably. Previously they had thought only of influencing from without; but now they understood they could reside deep within a human's spirit and exert their demonic influence from within. They revelled in the power that was theirs and grinned and chuckled as they considered the possibilities they saw for the future.

As it was explained to them, all they had to do was to bring temptation to bear, ensure it was acted on and open up those chinks in a human's spirit with bigger and better temptations, until there was enough sin and degradation present for a demon to enter. They now understood that small temptations might produce small chinks, which could allow a demon with a little power to enter and live within the person. However, if a human succumbed to much larger temptations then far more powerful demons could enter that life with correspondingly better results.

In his previous role as the "Bearer of the Light," Lucifer had overseen the ministries that the angelic host had provided for mankind and had in the process gained considerable insight into how humans thought and functioned. That knowledge was to be put to good use, as he explained to his demon commanders, where he was sure the weakest points in the human character lay. He had already instructed them concerning the more ambitious people's susceptibility to desiring power, more power and yet more power and how that characteristic could be encouraged and developed.

Now he expanded on an area of vulnerability to which he knew almost every human would be susceptible. He drew his audience close around him as he proceeded to inform them. He winked and sniggered and spoke in low tones as he changed the beauty of a wonderful gift into something that was base and dirty. He relayed how, once humans were in a fallen state, their sexual desires would quickly become the means by which they could easily be brought down. He told how the need for sexual gratification could be moved from its rightful place to illicit relationships.

Satan was now in full swing as he revelled in expanding

the influences that he and his demons could bring to bear. He detailed the perversions in which he saw human beings engage and his enthusiasm grew and spread to the demon commanders around him. He knew from their response that he had hit on a major method by which his purposes could be accomplished.

One of the most beautiful things that Earth contained was a parents' love for their children and the immensely strong bonding which that love produced. Now Satan would use his incredible intelligence to design ways in which the purity of that love and the strength of those relationships, might be perverted into a satanic stronghold. He had seen how his demons responded to him when he brought fear and corruption to bear on them and how through those strategies he was able to obtain the responses he desired.

The natural dependency and trust that existed between child and adult, was indeed a lovely thing. What if that relationship was corrupted through the imposition of unnatural sexual desires, implanted into the minds of the adults and they were to betray that trust by sexually abusing children? The point that really inspired him was the corruption of natural desires into action that ran completely counter to what the Creator had ever intended. When that happened it would be as though he, Satan, had become the creator and he revelled in that possibility, knowing that it could all be accomplished through temptation and fear.

So, he reasoned, if sufficient fear and corruption was brought to bear on humans, they would, just like his demons, do anything he wanted them to do and child abuse would become a reality. But, why not go beyond simple abuse into the very heart of the matter and create the most dreadful human behaviour of all, child sacrifice! He was sure he could do it. It was only a question of the amount of fear that could be engendered within parents. Was not the creation of fear one of his strongest assets? He saw a time when parents would, under the enormous pressure of fear that he would subject them to, surrender their children to the flames and watch as they were consumed as a sacrifice to a god of their imagination. He, Satan, would receive their sacrifice and delight in taking it to himself.

There was another aspect of child sacrifice that Satan resolved to bring into being and that was the destruction of human life, through the abortion of living foetuses. As the concept struck his mind, so his heart almost stopped, as he realised the destructive power of what he was conceiving. "Yes," he breathed out loud, "that's the way to go. I'll get them to destroy their own unborn children!"

As he spoke to the commanders of his demon army, Satan reflected on the contrast between the peace, serenity and order that he had known in Heaven, as the angel Lucifer and the violence and fear that were part of his recent interaction with them. He remembered clearly the culture of Heaven with the Father's love, pervading the very atmosphere and the joy and contentment that he and every angel had known for eons past. Out of his fallenness, a deep anger and hatred that emanated from the absolute core of his being, was directed against those memories and more especially what he knew still existed in the Kingdom of Heaven and upon the Earth.

Satan ground his teeth in a physical manifestation of

anger, revulsion and disgust and resolved there and then to bring lawlessness and violence upon the whole of creation. In his mind's eye he could see distress, lawlessness, destruction, famine, disease, poverty, violence and war upon the Earth and he longed for his desire's fulfilment. He also wanted the entire host of Heaven to be subject to him. He growled deep in his throat and swayed from side to side in anger as he resolved to establish these things upon the Earth and in the heavenly places.

The passion of hatred that these thoughts generated almost took over and in a moment of time, he retained control and brought his thoughts back to the task in hand. He paused momentarily, refocused his mind and continued with the briefing of his commanders. With them he strategised ways in which lawlessness and violence might be established and how these things would be used to further his purposes.

Satan had never really understood why the Father had given the gift of free will to both angels and humans. He had always struggled with the concept, but now that his mind was in the ultimate degenerate state, he had no use for such foolishness.

He would not be satisfied until he exercised absolute domination and control over all things; the very idea of any kind of freedom was an anathema to him. Satan had looked upon the human condition and seen how they debated their issues and used their freedom to decide on a particular choice or course of action. In his heart he had resolved that this situation was unacceptable to him because, he reasoned, absolute control and freedom were at the opposite ends of a continuum. The whole concept of freedom stood in opposition to the totalitarian regime that he was in the process of bringing into being, but how to eradicate freedom was the question with which he now wrestled?

He was in the process of thinking through exactly what freedom meant and was saying to himself that freedom was basically the ability to decide for oneself what particular course of action to take, in any particular situation and to be able to act on that decision. So, he reasoned, remove the ability for humans to decide for themselves and their freedom will be a thing of the past.

Suddenly Satan knew that addiction was the answer for which he was looking, because addiction removed the possibility of free will being exercised and put in its place an automated response to an unnatural need. He grinned slyly to himself knowing that he had come up with something that was going to be so powerful and ruinous in the lives of many, many humans.

Whilst he was considering who to select to run this part of his Strategic Plan, he pondered what other possibilities there were with regard to the loss of freedom. He looked upon his senior military officers, assembled before him and saw clearly that they were there to do his bidding, to come and go as he decreed and to obey exactly as he commanded. They had no freedom of choice; he controlled their entire lives.

The realisation suddenly dawned on him that they were actually nothing more than slaves! So why not use slavery as a major weapon in his destruction of personal freedom? He liked the idea. He closed his eyes and pictured a scene which had humans toiling away as slaves to other humans. The lash was being used almost indiscriminately and brutality, was in evidence everywhere. "Yes, that's the way to go," he quietly said to himself. He lost no time in designating a senior commander, General Obligato, to be the strong man and take charge of this particular sphere of operations.

It was as the Strategic Planning meeting came to an end that General Libidinous came to him and asked regarding the women of the human species. He had knelt before his Lord Satan with his helmet removed and all due supplication being made. The general was well known for his strong sexual desires and wanted to know if it was permissible for himself and those under his command to interact sexually with human women, whom he found particularly attractive. The general had made his case well and had clearly thought through the implications of what he was requesting. He made the point that through such unions, the genetic line of the human race could easily be corrupted. He pointed out that any progeny would be a combination of demon and human genes and how this combination would bring into being a whole new race that the Creator had not intended nor designed. He went on to suggest that this surreptitious course of action, might well undermine the whole of creation and allow his Lord Satan to have a significant influence over future human generations and the very course of human development.

Satan pondered this proposal seriously and warmed to the possibilities it suggested. The point he liked most was that it gave him an ability to not only be influential in the corruption of human kind, but the opportunity to create a race of beings that would be under his control, owe allegiance to him and not to the Father. In his fertile imagination, he saw what he thought they might possibly look like. He was sure they would be considerably larger than humans, with both human and demon characteristics. It pleased him that he could be absolutely certain that they would be spiritually and morally corrupt from the start, because of the degenerate seed from which they had been sired. The spiritual, psychological and physical possibilities excited him. He gave his approval to the scheme and General Libidinous sneered gratuitously at the thought of the pleasures that were soon to be his.

C6
THE FALL OF HUMANITY

Satan had decided that his initial goal was to become the ruler of the planet Earth. He was very aware that the Father had given that role to mankind but was determined to have it surrendered to him. For that to happen he knew he must first break the bond of perfect friendship that existed between the Father and the humans. The reconnoitering that he had done, had shown him that his best line of attack was through the female of the human species, who seemed to exert considerable influence over the male and yet he thought appeared more susceptible to the possibility of succumbing to temptation.

During his secret observation of the humans what had struck him was their innocence. This motivated them to always desire the best for each other and they seemed to be completely without malice. They lived in right relationship with each other and their Lord God, in a harmony and friendship that he found quite sickening. He had noted their zest for life and the fun and laughter that was so much part of them. They were fit and healthy and glowed with a radiance that bespoke a life of perfection. They lived a utopian existence that caused him to grind his teeth in anger and deepened his resolve to bring it to an end.

He thought long and hard to identify the real core of his subject. He decided that obedience was the central issue because the relationship of unity and harmony that existed between the Father and humanity was based upon it. Satan correctly deduced that the Lord God's sovereignty and authority and the humans' free will, were perfectly balanced. He was their God and they obeyed Him because they wanted to and chose to. If he could upset that balance and cause disobedience to occur, the perfection of their relationship would be broken.

He planned his attack carefully, realising that if he was to appear to the woman and speak temptation to her, he must change his form to something that was acceptable to the female of the species, would not frighten her and yet remained in character for him. He chose to become a serpent.

The other decision Satan had to make, concerned the nature and depth of temptation he would bring to bear upon the woman. His spies had overhead conversations that had taken place and he was aware that the only condition the Father had placed upon His human friends, was that they were to remain innocent, having no knowledge of good and evil. He decided to make the impartation of the knowledge of good and evil his primary objective.

His approach to the woman was both cunning and solicitous. After a little persuasion and the use of more than a little guile, coupled with a strong reassurance that this knowledge would not bring death, as the Father had suggested, but would actually give her the same wisdom concerning good and evil that the Father had, she agreed to receive it. As she did so, Satan was overcome with a delight that he could not fully contain and he spontaneously danced a wiggling jig to celebrate his success. The woman's next action went beyond what even he had dared to hope. Of her own volition she immediately went to her husband and shared her newfound knowledge with him; he also accepted it and took it to himself and so disobedience entered both of them.

The outward effect of their newly acquired knowledge was initially modest, to say the least. The humans became aware of their nakedness, which caused them to cover themselves and they missed their usual evening meeting with the Father, but Satan could discern little else. He had sat and pondered and finally reasoned out the full ramifications of what had occurred.

It seemed to him that whilst in the past the humans had been in receipt of the gift of free will, they had never actually used it to do anything that ran counter to what the Father wanted, although the potential for that had always existed. Now, he reasoned, they had actually crossed the line and disobeyed the Father. He glowed inwardly. They had decided to act in a way that was not in accordance with what the Father desired for them. They had acted independently and actually established their independence from Him. Even more than that, they had broken their bonding to the Father and were no longer able to live in His nearer presence, because of the contamination that was now upon them and was part of them.

Satan had once been holy and blameless and as the angel Lucifer, had full understanding of the principles of righteousness and how it could not mix with unrighteousness. So the humans' desire to remove themselves from the Father's presence came as no surprise to him. For he himself had been separated from the Father for precisely the same offence, the establishment of his own independence.

He began to realise how much the situation had changed and that if the humans were no longer in their safe haven and under the Father's protection, they would be in his world and completely exposed to his influence and the harassment of those under his command.

For some time now he had been carefully considering the suggestions that General Libidinous had made, concerning sexual interaction with human women and he was keen to explore and develop that concept.

Satan felt deep in his being that the Father's love for his creation, and in particular the humans, meant He would in the future, endeavour to bring them back to Himself and restore the relationship which they had broken. He allowed his mind to investigate the possible scenarios and he began to consider what was the worst that could happen. He had come to the conclusion that if men were raised up to speak against what he was doing, then he would simply influence the thinking of the hearers, so that they would not act on what they were being told. He knew he had forces and resources that could accomplish this. It was when he considered the absolute worst-case scenario that he felt his blood run cold and the very thought of it stopped him dead in his tracks.

He spoke out loud to himself, "No, He wouldn't!" But he knew deep in his black heart that the Father would. He stamped his feet and ground his teeth in anger and shouted a string of obscenities to give vent to his feelings. The realisation remained that when all else failed the Father would incarnate into the human race and speak personally to them, giving expression to His boundless love for them.

Satan had raised his head and with his horns pointing heavenward shouted at the sky, *"Well, I'll fix you. You'll be begging me for mercy by the time I've finished with you. This is now my world, my principality and I will rule it my way, you're finished here!"*

He felt better for his outburst but when he had regained his composure, knew that he had to act decisively if he was to win the battle that lay ahead. Muttering to himself he had continued to think the thing through, "For Him to incarnate He needs a pure genetic line, a blood line that's uncontaminated. He's never going to be willing to mix his holiness with anything that has my influence within it." With that thought Satan had thrown back his head and laughed in relief. "It's easy," he had chortled, "I've got the answer."

Immediately he had called all his generals to an Orders Group to issue fresh instructions to them. They again gathered before him and honoured him with their knees bent and their heads bowed. Satan left them in that uncomfortable position until he felt they had worshipped him adequately and were sufficiently conscious of the difference in status between them. Then he bade them stand and listen as he proceeded to give orders that were to put in place events, that would in time have a devastating consequence for the whole of mankind.

Drawing himself up to his full height he towered above his

generals and looking down on them he began to speak, "I am sure that you are all aware that I am a hard task master and I intend to remain so. You and those you command, I will deal with exactly as I please and your lives are mine to expend. However, if I choose to do so I can also be benevolent and reward exceptional service. In the battles that have taken place so far, you have all served me well and in the battles that lie ahead you may well give your life, if I require it."

He continued, "We are now entering a time of intense activity and I require you to be diligent in the assignment I am about to give you, but I think when you hear what it is you will agree it has some deeply satisfying and pleasurable aspects contained within it."

Satan paused to allow his words to penetrate some very thick skulls before continuing, "As your Commander in Chief, I am not in the habit of explaining my actions or reasons for them, but in this case I believe it is important that you understand the seriousness of the situation and how I have seen fit to handle it.

Due to the brilliant strategy that I devised and implemented, the humans are now no longer in a close relationship with the Father. Their alienation from Him has curtailed the special relationship they had." His voice rose in pitch and volume as he excitedly shouted, "And they have declared their independence from Him!"

The demon commanders rose to their feet as one and brandished their swords above their heads cheering loudly in a manifestation of wild enthusiasm for what they were being told. Satan was pleased that they had comprehended the significance of what he had said and allowed them to express their feelings for a while, before he motioned for them to settle down. When they were quiet and still he continued, "It is my considered opinion that despite the rebelliousness of the humans and their declaration of independence, the Father," and again he spat green bile and ground it in with his hind legs, "loves them deeply and will do whatever is necessary to restore them to Himself."

Satan paused to give his demons time to digest the magnitude of what he had just said and then continued, "One way, in which He may do this, is through the appointment of selected individuals who will speak His words telling them of His willingness to have them returned to a relationship with Him. If this happens our strategy will be to dull the minds of the people to prevent them from acting on what they are being told. When He fails, as surely He will, it is my belief that He will adopt an extreme strategy and personally incarnate into the human race, to show them how much he loves and cares for them." His voice had risen in volume and pitch but now he lowered it to a husky whisper, "If this happens, all the work I have done to bring about their separation will be wasted."

He then shouted at the top of his voice, ***"This I will not allow!"*** Then lowering his voice continued, "You and those under your command will ensure it does not happen! The way forward is for all of us to focus on one plan of attack, to the exclusion of everything else until we have achieved my primary goal. Are you ready for what I am about to tell you?" Their immediate and loudly shouted response of, "Yes, Lord Satan," assured him of their enthusiasm and attentiveness.

The demon commanders had been listening intently to what their Commander in Chief had been saying and knew from his sense of urgency and the expectation his words had been building, that this briefing had immense importance. Satan continued, "For Him to become a human being, He needs a pure blood line through and into, which to be born and that, we will deny Him. Do you understand what I am saying?"

In the front rank General Cruella shifted uncomfortably from one foot to the other. The furrows across his leathery forehead coupled with the expression around the fangs protruding from his lower jaw and the look in his yellow slit eyes, clearly said he was puzzled. The slight lowering of his massive bony head confirmed his distress. Satan's powers of observation rarely missed anything. He immediately saw the General's body language and correctly interpreted both the fact that there was something he did not understand along with his reluctance to express his puzzlement. He addressed the General in a low growl, "I am aware that this is an unusual and complex situation General Cruella and it is important that we all have a good grasp of the strategy I am explaining and will be using. What is it that you wish to say?"

General Cruella collapsed to his knees and lowered his forehead to the ground before he spoke, "I beg your mercy and indulgence, my Lord Satan, and humbly request your permission to ask a question."

Moving slowly towards him, Satan caused those around the General, who were unsure what vicious response might be forthcoming, to carefully distance themselves from him. "You have my permission General to ask a question," Satan replied, "but it had better be a good one!"

General Cruella inhaled deeply through his moist flared nostrils and summoning all the courage he possessed, said in his gravelly voice, "My Lord Satan I beg to ask why the Father, whom I loathe and hate, would risk becoming a human in a world that is now polluted both spiritually and physically." He paused before inhaling another deep breath and continuing, "Is He not, my Lord, putting Himself at considerable risk in laying aside His power and glory to become a man? Does He not, my Lord, become susceptible to the possibility of temptation, and in His humanity, is there not the inevitability of death?" Having asked his questions, General Cruella became silent and remained perfectly still as he awaited his Master's response, which he hoped would not bring about his own execution. He held his breath and closed his eyes in preparation for what might come.

Satan looked down at General Cruella and realised that this was a good opportunity to inform his senior demons of the situation as he saw it and to demonstrate his superior grasp of the theological facts. Putting on the most benevolent appearance he could, he spoke, "You have asked an important question, General Cruella, and I will give you an answer but before I do you may rise and rejoin your colleagues." General Cruella felt the power of relief wash over him as he rose gratefully to his feet and stepped back into the line of military commanders, who closed ranks about him again, accepting him back into their number, now the danger of being hurt by the overflow of Satan's reprisal appeared to have past.

"The situation is this." Satan began, "The crux of the matter is what He calls love, a quality that none of us here either have, or want, and therefore it is difficult to comprehend. However, it is important that you all do your best to grasp what I am about to say because then you can position your forces where they can be most effective and do the most damage." He paused and signalled for them to be seated, which he did, not so much out of consideration for their comfort, but more because he now towered over them, giving him an increased psychological advantage.

He continued, "The fact is, whether you comprehend it or not the Father loves His creation and especially those miserable creatures we know as humans. Under my incredibly powerful tempting influence they have now exercised their free will in opposition to the Father's will for them. That, I am delighted to say, has resulted in their having an understanding of good and evil. I have stripped their protective innocence from them and because they are now contaminated by sin they have become part of my kingdom and are therefore under my influence. He has had no option but to exclude them from His nearer presence, because His disgusting holiness and righteousness cannot mix with their wonderful sinfulness." He paused for effect and chuckled gleefully revelling in what he had been able to achieve. The demon commanders rattled their swords against their shields in appreciation and Satan smiled slyly.

When Satan opened his mouth to again speak, the sword rattling stopped instantly and Satan continued, "The love that I mentioned the Father has for His creation may produce an unprecedented response from Him. It is because He craves fellowship with the humans that He stupidly made in His own likeness. Another great weakness He has is towards being forgiving and I strongly believe this will cause him to take the extreme step of incarnating into His creation as a human."

Satan looked about scanning the faces of his commanders, estimating their understanding of the colossal statement he had just made. Satisfied by the stunned silence he continued, "This will be to speak to them personally and to reveal His love for them, in an effort to restore them to relationship with Him. To do that He needs a pure genetic bloodline and this we will deny Him!"

Satan again paused to allow the magnitude of what he had just said to penetrate before continuing, "Now, this is the part you are all going to enjoy. What my entire force is going to do, under your supervision, is to copulate with the females of the human species and seriously contaminate their genetic make-up. I require a race of beings to walk the Earth that is a human-demon hybrid. In this way we will breed out the human race and so eliminate the possibility of His incarnation."

In the baseness of their imaginations the demons began living the experiences that were soon to be theirs. Sniggering broke out amongst them with some nudging those around them in suggestive ways. Others began to laugh hideously and slap their comrades on the back by way of congratulation. As Satan watched this performance he smiled inwardly. He knew that he had carried his commanders with him and that the fulfilment of his scheme was assured. He coughed loudly several times to regain their attention and restore order before he continued, "My observation of the female of the human species brings me to believe they are fickle and for whom appearance is of significant importance. I do not believe they will find you attractive in your present form. Therefore, I require you to change the way you look and assume a handsome human male appearance before showing yourselves to them. I do not want them traumatised, but willing to succumb to your advances."

Satan paused to allow his words to be digested and then narrowing his eyes and speaking more quietly and gently than he had ever done before, continued in a vein that he knew would run counter to every tenant and fiber of a demon's being. The softness of his voice gained the senior commander's attention like nothing else could and was in such contrast to how Satan normally spoke, that they were all ears when he said, "You are to speak nicely to them and be attentive to their every need. In this way they will soon accept you and be compliant to your every desire. The offspring that you sire, will be the foundation of a redesigned human race, that will corrupt the genetic line. Instead of them being in His image they will be in our image and He will never be willing to incarnate into such a beautifully corrupt and distorted version of His creation."

Feeling very satisfied with his explanation Satan looked around. The scene in front of him began to change dramatically and now instead of demon commanders, he was looking at a very different assembly of beings, as they prepared themselves for their new and pleasurable assignment.

C7

NEPHILIM

It did not take long for the human women to accept their handsome and attentive suitors, who paid them compliments and were so polite and gentle. Courtship was carried out with flowers and gifts in profusion, female heads were turned and hearts won throughout the human race. The women were proud of their new partners and enjoyed immensely the attention and compliments they received.

The new men in the women's lives were considerably larger and more handsome than the normal human male and in due course they began bearing their children. The women were delighted with their offspring and many a "baby show" took place, as their hearts were warmed and their lives fulfilled by the apparent blessings that had come upon them.

As the children grew it became obvious that all was not well, for some became so large as to be considered giants. There were others that were strange and very different in appearance to their parents. Some were being born with physical abnormalities as the result of the mix of human and demon genes. There were the one eyed giants and the part animal part human creatures, those that had wings and those with supernatural abilities, that allowed them to demonstrate powers normal humans did not have. New life forms were coming into being as the result of the sexual unions between the demons and the human women; life forms that had not been designed by the Father and which had spiritual corruption deep within them.

Other defects began to surface in the social structure of this hybrid society. As time passed, changes were becoming apparent in the characters of the males and their veneer of niceness and respectability began to wear thin. Their demonic characteristics started to show through and they became irritable and difficult to live with.

The first violent incident was a complete and total shock to the woman concerned, that ran beaten, blooded, distraught and crying from her house to the home of a neighbour. She had expected support from the friend and her husband, but neither woman could comprehend his belligerent attitude and wholehearted endorsement for what had occurred. The beating he gave his wife for good measure left her injured, shocked, traumatised and uncomprehending of his actions.

This initial act of violence acted as a trigger. It set off a chain reaction that erased the veneer of caring, civilised behaviour under which the demons had been functioning. The social scene changed rapidly, and where love and affection had once been, now hatred and violence became the norm.

The Father saw what was happening and His heart was grieved. He became aware how corrupt and sinful His creation had become. He had known from the beginning how risky it was to give the gift of free will to angels and humans. He had done it because He knew that unless they related to Him from choice, the relationship had no value and was quite worthless.

He looked at the violence that was taking place and the strange creatures that He had neither designed nor created and saw that even some of the animals had been corrupted through bestiality. There were now those that were part animal and part human. He regretted bringing mankind into being and resolved to do something about the evil and corrupt creatures He now looked upon.

Yet, in all this darkness and despair there was one pinpoint of light, which pleased His heart and gave Him hope. In amongst all the genetic distortion and pollution, spiritual corruption and physical violence, He was aware of a small group of humans that had refused to have anything to do with the new social structure that had come into being. They had kept themselves uncontaminated by the Nephilim. They had remained in fellowship with Him and free from the evil that was all around them. He counted them and they numbered eight, a small family, but sufficient for what He had in mind.

Apart from that one family, what He now saw on the Earth was not really His creation but a seriously modified and demonic version of it. His righteous anger came to the fore and He made the decision to wipe out and destroy all life on the Earth, apart from that one small family and the lineage of uncorrupted animals. He would cleanse the Earth, remove from it all that was evil and corrupt and repopulate it using their uncontaminated genetic seed.

The Father pondered the situation and thought about how

He would bring about the cleansing of the Earth. He decided to use water, turning the Earth's vapour into droplets and causing it to fall upon its surface as rain. He would do this in such magnitude, as to cause a flood, which would drown all life. But how to preserve the small family and the animal life? They needed a safe haven, a place into which they could retreat whilst the waters were covering the Earth and a boat was the obvious answer. However, a boat of the size and type that would be needed did not exist. Would the small family be sufficiently obedient to build one? The Father decided to find out.

The Father spoke to the leader of the family and told him exactly what to do, specifying the dimensions of the craft and precisely how it was to be constructed. Also, telling him the numbers of animals that were to go into the boat with them. Then the Father waited.

Immediately the small family went to work and the Father blessed their efforts. Trees were cut and materials gathered and the boat started to take shape. The work happened against a background of ribald remarks made by the Nephilim around them who gathered to watch the construction take place. They had started by asking what the family was doing and when told that a large boat was being built because rain was coming that would flood the Earth; they had fallen about laughing and spent their time ridiculing the boat builders and making jokes at their expense.

It was hard work but the small family toiled ceaselessly to complete the task. When the boat was finally finished the Father acted supernaturally and brought to it the animals that were also to be saved. When they and the small family were safely inside, He closed the large door for them and then they were safely cocooned in their self-contained world.

The humans had never been close to so many animals, but they were aware of the Father's supernatural influence by the way the animals had willingly come aboard of their own volition. Despite their natural tendencies they seemed to readily accept both the humans and each other.

Speaking to the creation, the Father commanded that all the outlets beneath the Earth and the floodgates of the sky above should open. The effect of His words was immediate as the sky started to form clouds. At first they were small, puffy and white but quickly grew and darkened until they became black and menacing.

The thick heavy clouds caused the day to darken and become grey and brooding. Then a streak of lightning arced across the sky and the first clap of thunder sounded menacingly over the land, its voice echoed from valley to valley and across the hills. Like the beat of mighty battle drums, the thunder rolled and boomed, reverberating and shaking the sky. Over the land the lightning speared, parried and thrust into the soft belly of the vulnerable earth. The thunder crashed again and again. Sheet lightning lit the sky, illuminating the outline of the hills in a ghostly glow. Quickly, the fork lightning that followed, lit up the day and sent massive electrical discharges impacting into the atmosphere, charging the ether with its power. The Earth was pricked and speared by electrical thrusts that penetrated and damaged at the point of impact, vaporising the ground's surface as if cauterising a wound.

New storms began in other parts of the sky. They competed

with each other in flinging the most powerful thunderbolts and to crash and bang the loudest. Their lightning's outperformed each other in arcing, flashing, forking and sheeting. The storms grew in intensity and brilliance and filled the sky with spectacular displays of raw electrical power of an awe-inspiring magnitude.

From the sky to the ground the stage was set and the storms performed a presentation of cataclysmic dimensions. They flashed and boomed whilst moving in an atmospheric dance that battled and whirled until the gaps between them closed, their edges touched and intertwined as they joined forces to terrify the Earth.

The falling rain, that started as a descending mist, became gentle droplets that grew in size until they splashed and sploshed with a heavy fullness that brought massive quantities of water from the Earth's atmosphere onto its surface, wetting everything, soaking and drenching without respite. The water spouts from beneath the Earth combined with the rain. The resulting puddles grew until they became ponds and the ponds became lakes that deepened and broadened, becoming a sea that covered the land.

The gentle breeze became a wind that grew in intensity and strengthened until it howled like a banshee portending death, whilst cursing the land and its inhabitants. Its physical force was not easily resisted as it pushed and pulled, grasping and grabbing at plants and trees, tearing and uprooting. It tore and smashed its way from place to place, as if knowing that nothing could withstand its onslaught. It lifted foliage and broken trees high into the air and carried them away in its powerful swirling grasp. The sound of its roar deepening as its velocity increased.

The people and creatures of the Earth were surprised and then shocked by the change in their environment. The rain quickly soaked them and the wind chilled and bullied them. The thunder and lightning struck fear deep into them, causing panic as it continued unabated and grew in frequency and magnitude.

As the water deepened so did the people's distress. They made their way to higher ground and when the water continued to rise, those that were nimble, climbed trees whilst many went to the boat and banged on its sides begging to be let in. The water became deeper still and the boat began to move slightly and then to float and the people around it panicked and beat harder upon it, but to no avail. They clung to its sides, screaming and crying.

Inside the boat the small family listened intently to all that was going on outside and tried to remain calm and detached. The sound of distraught people beating upon their safe haven, tore at the small family's heartstrings but their commission was clear and they knew they were to do nothing to assist them. After the water had risen sufficiently and the boat had rocked several times and floated free of its moorings, those outside clinging to it, tired and lost their grip. Their shouts and screams silenced as they were washed away and drowned. The demons inhabiting their bodies were released as they died.

The pounding water grabbed at the boat, spinning it round and lashing it with its fury. It ducked and bobbed in the water, acquiescing to the storm's power and strength but its buoyancy ensured it remained on the surface. Its strong timbers protected the small family and the animals from any harm, keeping them safe and dry.

The storm also tested the humans' courage and if the Father had not made a covenant with them, they may well have succumbed to fear and panic. They knew that what was occurring was His will and that they had a role to play. They had witnessed and experienced the violence of the Nephilim and the distortions that had overtaken the human race and understood the cleansing the Father was now carrying out.

The water rose steadily and the storm outside continued for a long time. Inside the boat everything was warm and dry and the small family came to terms with their new environment and began to take stock of what the Father had entrusted to them.

They had always known that the Earth had a variety of animal life but had seen only a small portion of it. Now they were living in close proximity and harmony with it all and they marvelled at its complexity and diversity. They were able to examine at close quarters the various textures and colours of skin and fur.

They could see how some creatures were sleek and streamlined and had been designed for speed, whilst others moved slowly and had superb strength and camouflage. Some animals had cloven hooves, that were ideal for walking on rocks and hard surfaces, whilst those that swam had webbed feet. Animals that ate the foliage of tree branches high off the ground had long necks and others long snouts for getting into ants' nests.

They were all wonderful to behold and the humans had many conversations and discussions as they observed and marvelled at the animals with whom they now shared their lives and for whose preservation they had been made responsible.

There was much for the small family to do concerning the care of themselves and the animals and they quickly established a routine. Each day they prepared food, gave thanks, grateful for the sanctity the boat provided and ate together. They also fed the animals from the supplies they had brought on board and cleaned a portion of their new home.

Day, followed day and still the rain continued flooding the land. Valleys, hills and then mountains disappeared into its swirling grasp and beneath its turbulent surface.

After many days the wind began to drop and the rain lessened. The sky lightened and a weak sun appeared above them. When finally the rain had stopped completely and the sunshine warmed the boat the small family welcomed its return by singing and dancing on the deck and rejoicing together. With grateful hearts they praised and worshipped the Father and thanked Him for their lives and the lives of the animals onboard.

The small family had realised from the beginning that their lives were in the Father's hands and that His sovereignty was over them. Although what was occurring was almost completely beyond their understanding they were very aware that they were flowing with the Father's will and knowing this, gave them confidence and allowed them to relax.

As they looked out from the boat all they could see was water in every direction. Its surface had now become calm and placid and they waited knowing that it would recede and land would again appear.

Eventually their patience was rewarded and mountain peaks began to poke above the water. After many more days of watching the water subside and seeing more and more land coming into view their boat came to rest once more upon dry land.

They were high up in a range of mountains but so grateful to be alive, well and safe that they willingly gave thanks from the bottom of their hearts to the God who had preserved them. The small family waited for the water to recede still further before opening the big door and releasing the animals back into the outside environment to begin the process of repopulating the Earth.

C 8

CONSEQUENCES

The Father's destruction of the Nephilim was a major blow to Satan's plans. He had ground his teeth in fury when he realised the Creator's determination to prevent the physical manifestation of his demonic presence in the human race but all was not lost.

In the same way that genetic defects can be passed from generation to generation through the genes of parents into their children, so spiritual contamination can be passed-on in a similar way. The ground that humans had given to the demonic before the flood now stood as an entry point into all their lives.

The temptation to which they had succumbed provided the opening that allowed demonic infiltration to enter and affect every aspect of their character and behaviour. Satan was determined to exploit to the full the advantage he had gained. He made it very clear to his minions that whenever possible, the creative work of the Father was to be undermined and anything the Father valued was to be contaminated or destroyed.

Satan was very aware that humans had been created in the Father's image and therefore the corruption of their characters was one of his top priorities. Not only that, but because the Father valued human life so much, the devaluing of human life and the denigration of its intrinsic value was most important to him. He stood in opposition to the Father and to the Father's will, values and ethics. Whatever the Father valued he endeavoured to devalue and whatever the Father blessed he sought to curse.

Even the 'small family' was not immune from the effects of their ancestor's dalliance with evil and although their contamination was simply through them belonging to a fallen race, still they were part of a genetic line that was spiritually defective. Each of them had been born into corruption and all their offspring had within them the effects of it. Satan knew that he had won a major victory when he originally planted the seed that had borne the fruit of independence, independence from the Father. Now he was determined to fertilise that seed and cause it to grow into a destructive force, that would align the human race totally with him and his corrupt purposes, so that he gained total power and dominion over them.

Satan reasoned correctly, then they would willingly do his will and move away from any relationship with the Father and the righteousness and holiness that were intended by the Father for them. Their allegiance would be to him, the Lord Satan, and their membership firmly established in his evil kingdom. They would submit their wills and bow the knee to him, giving to him the deference and worship he craved and effectively making him their god and the ruler of their world. Any relationship with the Father would soon be lost and membership of the Father's Kingdom would become nothing more than a distant memory and would eventually be forgotten. Then he, Satan, would reign supreme in their world and in their lives.

Time passed and the 'small family' multiplied and human beings again spread across the surface of the earth. They built dwellings and villages, towns and cities. Nations formed and cultures were established and national identities came into being, as the human race developed and grew. New skills were learned and professions, trades and occupations became expressions of their inherent intelligence, gifts and natural abilities.

From the beginning, it was apparent that subversive influences were again making themselves felt. The demons delighted in exploiting the ground they had gained many years before when those first humans had succumbed to temptation and decided to exercise their free will, in opposition to the will of the Father and to live independently from Him. That independence became the right of passage the demons had to influence and tempt, to enter-in and corrupt and wherever possible, to possess and control human beings.

The demons quickly became skilled at finding those who lusted after power and were strongly motivated to cruelly dominate others. They sought out such people and empowered them, living within them and strengthening the negative aspects of their characters. They spoke into their minds and enhanced the natural aggressive qualities those people had. Continuing this process until their character defects had been honed to a fine cutting edge of selfish ambition, domination and cruelty.

Satan looked upon the situation of sin and corruption he

saw rapidly developing and leered with satisfaction. He knew the time was ripe for him to put in place the plan that would ensure the worship he craved would come to him and not go to the Father. He had given this part of his strategy very careful consideration and had already decided on the demon that would give him the best chance of success. He wanted no angelic interference and went to great lengths to be sure they would not overhear his plans as he briefed this principle player.

He used a very minor demon to act as his messenger; no angel would ever guess the importance of the task he was giving to Apprenticus, the most junior of demons, who was not even a member of Satan's personal staff. Satan put nothing in writing but gave simple verbal instructions to the young demon, "Find Septicus and tell him I require to meet with him immediately at this location..."

They met on the shores of a volcanic lake with the smell of sulphur strong in their nostrils. The growl of satisfaction could be clearly heard as Septicus, a huge and powerful demon, received instructions from his Master. Twilight was giving way to the darkness of night, a time of day with which demons were most comfortable. The night covered their deceptive activities and gave them a degree of support not always offered by daylight. To be selected for a special task would give Septicus increased status with his compatriots. He puffed out his chest in pride, as he heard what was required of him and the privilege that was to be his.

Satan bent low and whispered in Septicus' ear in hushed tones and the air of camaraderie this instilled, made him feel very much at one with his Lord and Master. The foulness of the breath of the most corrupt and evil force in the universe, was like the caress of affection to him as he listened intently to the instructions he would gladly and willingly receive.

Septicus' sharp mind was quick to grasp the significance of what he was being told and Satan made it all sound so deliciously rewarding. The solicitous tone of Satan's voice came to him confidentially, as they shared the strategy that would move the human race once more into a depth of spiritual corruption, from which Satan intended it would never recover.

Satan regaled Septicus with flattery, regarding his value to him and thus drew him compliantly into his plans. "This is a role in which your maleness can really be used and fulfilled," he heard Satan say, "and the woman I have selected for you to copulate with, I'm sure you will find most delightful. She is very beautiful, with considerable experience in the art of lovemaking. Her name is Jazbeel, and she is in the fullness of the bloom of womanhood; she has a husband, but is very dissatisfied with his sexual performance.

You, Septicus are to come to her in the night when her husband is away and she desires a man and you are to make her pregnant. The progeny she will produce, will serve me in a most important way. I know that I can rely on you, Septicus." Septicus felt his maleness being aroused at the very thought of what he was hearing and he was quick to assure Satan of his willingness to do his bidding.

"You honour me, my Lord," Septicus growled gratuitously, "and I live only to serve you," he intoned solicitously as he ran his salivating tongue across his lips, causing the warts around his mouth to glisten in the moonlight, "I will comply with your orders absolutely, for I seek only to serve and to please you, my Master."

Satan continued his briefing, "Your present form is quite unacceptable for the task at hand and you are to assume the form of a handsome human male. Go now and comply with my orders and do not forget that I reward good work and punish failure savagely!" Septicus bowed low, his bony head nearing the ground as he paid homage before departing.

Satan knew that he had chosen wisely in selecting Septicus for this assignment and felt the corrosive satisfaction of one who had put in place a plan of action that would assuredly allow him to achieve his next and most evil strategic goal.

Septicus followed precisely the orders he had been given and in due course a son was born to Jazbeel and the child was named, Nimrod. His genes were such that he was two-thirds demon and one-third human and once again a demon-human hybrid, a Nephilim, had come into being.

As Nimrod grew to maturity, it was very obvious that he was different from those around him and Satan fostered those differences. Nimrod's natural inclinations strongly favoured the demonic and the character defects that he displayed, showed him to be his father's son. Septicus looked upon him with pride and Satan personally spent a great deal of time with him 'in the spirit,' encouraging and developing an ambitious, corrupt and vicious thought-life that would ultimately produce the results Satan wanted.

The Great Flood had occurred just a hundred years before, as the Lord God had cleansed the Earth of Nephilim. Now the problem was occurring again. Satan was careful not to overplay his hand and severely limited the number of Nephilim he allowed to be born. He had already experienced the destruction of his previous efforts and had no wish for a repeat performance.

Satan knew that a new strategy was necessary and for some time he had been thinking and pondering the shape and magnitude it might take. Suddenly he knew he had the answer! He again summoned Septicus to him and this time he ordered that they meet on the side of an active volcano, with its roar in the background to cover their words from angelic ears and with a light ash falling around them Satan received the oblations from Septicus that he considered his right.

A stream of molten lava moved slowly past them and they could feel its heat as it ran down the volcano's side, burning, demolishing and submerging everything in its path. The symbolism of its unstoppable destructive progress, was not lost on Satan and it acted as a visual representation of his intentions.

The Master Strategist drew his black cloak around his cloven form and became almost invisible in the half-light.

With no moon and the orange glow of the lava providing the only illumination, he looked down on Septicus kneeling before him and glowed inwardly at receiving the great demon's worship. He felt contentment at what he was about to bring into being. Keeping his voice low to maintain the secrecy of their meeting he spoke in a hushed whisper, his gravelly voice barely audible, "You may kiss my feet and rise," he intoned as Septicus gave to him the homage that he demanded. The strong sulphurous smell coming from the volcano did little to mask the stench emitted by Satan and Septicus, but in their own company they hardly noticed it. Septicus touched Satan's feet with his wart-encrusted lips, that enclosed his thick leathery tongue and then stood before his Master.

"You may be grateful that I am not displeased with your efforts so far," Satan said, "now, I am going to allow you to be part of a master strategy that will insidiously engulf the whole of human society to bring the human race under my influence and control in a far more complete and total way." Septicus had the intelligence and shrewdness to immediately express his gratitude and bowed his head whilst saying, "Thank you my Master. I live only to serve you." Satan's response was immediate, "Yes you do," he said sardonically, "and don't ever forget it or I'll boil you alive in oil and feed your carcass to the vultures. Now listen carefully, for I have no wish to repeat myself."

For the next hour Septicus listened intently as Satan outlined his plan for the spiritual downfall of the human race. Detailing how humans would come to worship, honour and obey him, the most evil and corrupt being in the universe. Septicus was amazed and delighted at the depth of planning that had gone into his Master's strategy.

Septicus heard how spiritual deviance could be constructed, to cater for everyone and every conceivable spiritual taste. Featuring high on the list was the overt worship of false gods, with a pantheon of them being brought into being to which men and women would bow and worship. Gods of stone, metal and wood; gods of the sun, moon and stars; gods of the forest and of the storm; gods of war and of child sacrifice; gods that required immorality and sexual perversion; gods that could be appeased only if virgin females were sacrificed to them;

gods of witchcraft that allowed people to manipulate spiritual forces for their own amusement and enrichment by providing wealth, fame and power in exchange for the worship of them; gods of humanism that encouraged the belief that humans were themselves gods, and so the list went on.

Septicus learnt how behind each deviant spiritual practice there was to be a high-ranking demon responsible for the development of that particular subterfuge, with a support structure of lesser demons under their command. These 'strong men' were also to be conduits, through which the praise and worship of the false gods was to be channelled immediately and directly to their master, Satan.

Satan again spoke to Septicus. His voice carried within it the low tones of secrecy and confidentiality; against which the subtle hiss of the molten lava running past them, Septicus had to concentrate and listen hard to what he was being told. Softly, Satan said, "I care not to whom humans worship and give their spiritual obeisance, so long as it is not Him!" He spat green bile into the passing molten lava and watched it as it was cooked and evaporated by the heat. He went on, "I will starve Him of the relationship for which He created these miserable human creatures and they will honour and worship me, not Him!"

Satan lifted his head and from deep within came a coarse and savage explosive laughter, that had in it the contempt that he felt for the God of the universe and the human race. Septicus willingly gave his assent to what he was hearing and joined his Master in ridiculing both the Lord of Life and human beings. The sound of their hellish fun and their demonic cackling rose to a crescendo of hatred and vengeance, as their mirthless expressions gave vent to the frustration and ambition that welled up from deep within these depraved and irredeemable beings.

When he had regained a measure of self-control Satan spoke again to Septicus, "I require someone whose loyalty and dedication to me is absolutely beyond question, to be in total command of this new and critically important initiative." He paused for effect and to allow the massive demon to digest the magnitude of what he was saying. Then he fixed Septicus with a focused and piecing stare that would have melted steel and which forced Septicus to look into his black bottomless eyes, as he held him in an almost hypnotic embrace of demonic power.

"I intend appointing you, Septicus, to this critically important position, but be very aware that if you should fail me in any way, I will ensure that eternity for you will have within it more pain than you can imagine. Do I make myself absolutely clear?" Septicus understood with crystal clarity what Satan was saying and felt within him a mixture of emotion. On the surface was pride and elation at being given this most important appointment, but underneath the delight was a deep-seated fear of what would befall him should he in any way fail.

Satan saw Septicus' countenance change and knew that he had engendered fear deep within him and was satisfied that he had created the correct foundation for his ongoing dominance of the great demon.

Now he was ready to give Septicus some special instructions to be complied with absolutely. He moved closer to Septicus until they were almost in contact with each other, this invaded the demon's personal space and produced in him a very uncomfortable feeling. Satan lifted his right cloven hoof and lowered it onto Septicus' left foot, then pivoted forward until all his weight was on it. The resulting pain that Septicus experienced was excruciating and he involuntarily emitted a low moan. Satan ignored this sound of his distress and turned his body to the right, in a vicious movement that was designed to significantly intensify the pain that Septicus was experiencing. Then he spoke directly into the demon's large, leathery and blackhead-infested ear, "Listen carefully," he said, "there will come a time when I firmly believe He will incarnate into the human race. He will have to do that through a human woman who has not known a man and is as pure as virgin snow. If my assumptions are correct and they usually are, He will use the power of His Spirit to make her pregnant. In this way His incarnation will not be contaminated by the corruption and filth I am implanting in the human race. This is really the only way He can accomplish what I believe He will decide to do."

As Satan paused to draw breath his vicious nature compelled him to twist his hoof a little more and press down with increased intensity. Septicus felt as though the bones in his foot were about to break. He wanted only to push his assailant away and draw his sword in retaliation, but knew that to oppose his Master in any way would result in him being cut to ribbons, by the flash of a lightning fast sabre he would probably not even see. He gritted and ground his teeth and exercised more self-control than he knew he had and hung on.

Septicus half closed his eyes as the pain reached a pinnacle of intensity and concentrated on remaining quite still. He again smelt the putrid breath that enveloped him as Satan breathed out and he had to stop breathing for a moment or he knew he would gag. Now Satan's voice became gritty and compelling as he spoke directly into his ear, "You are to establish in all principle societies, a tradition of virgin birth and the worship of the goddess and her child. Then, if He does as I suspect, it will be easy to discredit his actions as non-original and having been borrowed from elsewhere. Also, the seed will have been sown for me to simply shift the emphasis from the incarnation to the mother and cause those stupid humans not to worship Him alone."

Here the Master Strategist paused and thought aloud for a moment, "And then the worship comes to me!" Satan chuckled deep in his throat and in doing so sprayed Septicus with rotund droplets of dark green saliva, that smelt strongly of decaying flesh. He continued, "This is a most important part of my strategy, so be sure to carry out my wishes precisely or your present discomfort will seem as nothing more than a trifling tickle." Through gritted teeth Septicus just managed to speak his compliance with a pain filled, "Yes, my Lord." Then he felt the pain ease as Satan lifted his hoof with a sniggering laugh and left him staring at a black sooty emission, as the Vicious Protagonist sped elsewhere to plot and scheme.

The commission that Septicus had been given ensured he was influential in the spiritual development of a considerable number of myths, legends and deceptions spread over a long period of time. Septicus and his minions did their work well and it was through their efforts that these lies took root in all major cultures as they came to prominence. In ancient Babylon it was Nimrods wife, Semiramus, that was said to have conceived her child Tammuz without male fertilisation. In the Egyptian culture it was Isis and her son Osiris, in ancient Greece Venus and her child, Adonis.

Nimrod was born as the great grandson of Noah and carried the status appropriate to his human lineage. From another perspective he had been sired by a high-ranking demon and the genetic mix produced significant physical strength and great leadership ability, combined with a strongly satanic character and spirituality. He was of great importance to Satan, for he had the power to corrupt humans and to move the alignment of their spirituality away from the Living God towards the worship of him, the Great Deceiver. This, Nimrod did most willingly and effectively as he hunted for the souls of men and women.

Nimrod applied a strategy that centered humans in their own ability, aligning the focus for their well-being and happiness on themselves, away from any dependence on the Father. Through Nimrod a whole series of occultist practices were initiated that were born of the spirit of hatred and revenge, for Nimrod was determined to avenge the flood that had destroyed his kind.

The first thing that Satan needed was a firm base through which occult practices and thereby the worship of himself could take place. Nimrod's initial task was to build cities that contained temples to false gods to enable the fickle minds of humans to be turned away from the worship of the Father to the worship of deities that were borne of their own imaginings.

Nimrod was an immensely powerful character, with satanically given intelligence and charisma. So much so, that he accomplished his tasks with the acclaim of the people ringing in his ears. They fêted him and he became a great hero. Satan and the mind-controlling power of well organised demonic assistance moved the people's thinking in the direction in which the Great Corrupter wanted it to go.

After the Great Flood had subsided the Father had told the 'small family' what He wanted them to do. "Multiply and fill the Earth," He had said to them. Now Satan was ensuring that did not happen, as cities were built and the human population was contained within them. Again the Corrupter was standing in opposition to the will of the Father and influencing the human race to achieve what he wanted.

The methods by which Nimrod attained his aims were evil indeed. His character was so filled with the demonic and the forces of Hell were so deep within him, that he dealt ruthlessly with those who were subject to him. He quickly became a mighty despot who crushed those who opposed him. His influence over those who aligned with him brought them strongly into the satanic realm which he fostered and promoted.

To cleanse the land of the last vestiges of righteousness, Nimrod assembled a fighting force that had the capacity to invade the land adjacent to where he was based, thus uniting the entire territory under his banner of corruption. Then he built cities, with Babylon, Nineveh and others forming a firm base to foster a demonic spirituality. False gods became powerful in the lives of the people. Demons found fertile ground that they were able to easily inhabit as they claimed territory both geographically and spiritually. In this way, human society became subject to them.

At the same time whole industries grew up within these cities to satisfy the spiritual desires that had developed. Metal workers gained their livelihood by supplying what was required to sustain these false religions and they cast bronze, silver and gold images of false gods. Architects and stonemasons were much in demand for the design and building of edifices to pagan deities and Satan glowed with delight as the whole fabric of society moved in his direction and away from the worship of the Creator of the Universe.

Vast sums of money were spent building temples and shrines to false deities and there were many such places within each of the cities. Nor did Satan ignore the moral degradation he was able to foster with the introduction of temple prostitution. Here a man was able to come into full sexual union with a priestess of Ishtar, the goddess of love, and in that way be joined to the goddess, honouring her both spiritually and physically.

Demons moved through these spiritual entry points and established their presence in the lives of the people, taking and inhabiting whatever ground they gained and influencing and changing human spirituality; thereby the very fabric of society.

The strength of Satan's religious influence in the lives of people was based on fear. Fear that they would not have enough to eat because they had not worshipped the false deity enough, so the harvest might fail through lack of rain or pestilence. Fear that storms would come and destroy the crops. Fear that they would be attacked and taken into slavery by a powerful enemy. Fear they would be overrun and killed. Fear and worry was implanted into the human mind at every opportunity. Satan had whole legions of mind influencing demons working round the clock to bring human thought patterns into an alignment that would allow the maximum penetration of the human psyche by his demonic agents.

Fear, as Satan was very aware, is an insidious influence and once it had gained a foothold, has the capacity to grow like a cancer and take over whole areas of a person's, or a community's, life. It quickly became Satan's 'tool of trade' and with it he fashioned a complete religious structure, that filled the spiritual void in the people who did not have faith in the Living God.

So many fears were induced that it was not long before a whole pantheon of gods were being worshipped. Satan was very astute and quick to realise that in the realm of the spirit only two realities exist. Either worship is towards the Father or it is directed to a false god, behind which he stands. In this way, Satan was in reality the false god with the worship going to him and he revelled in what was happening and delighted in receiving the praise and worship of subjugated people; as they entered into bondage to him through their religious practices.

In the meantime, Nimrod excelled and grew in statue as he completed the tasks for which he had been brought into being. Within each of the cities that he built was a ziggurat. This was a huge stepped structure that reached up into the heavens and honoured the god of the city. In Babylon this was Marduk and a temple was constructed on top of the ziggurat in his honour.

The people now had an edifice that could be seen from anywhere in the city and by approaching travellers. The Father remained unseen by human eyes, but these great towers, topped by a temple, dominated the skyline and could be seen by all. This very largely removed the element of faith that was so necessary, if one was to live in relationship with an invisible

God. The gods that Nimrod brought into being, were not invisible and faith in their existence was not necessary, for they could be seen and touched and a person could worship any number of them. Everyone knew who the god of the city was, could see the temple and knew where they must go to worship.

The political arena was a special target and the demons gave it a great deal of attention. They quickly appreciated that here their influence could be most effective, for it was within the political setting that power over humans was established and legalised. If they brought uncaring and brutal despots to positions of political dominance and power, then the subversion and destruction of societies and nations was assured.

Another major consideration, was the value that the Father placed on human life and human beings. He saw them as the pinnacle of His creation having made them in His own image, they were designed to be a reflection of Himself. He had created them with a soul that comprised a mind, with which to think and which was equipped with a memory to recall the past; an imagination to envisage the future and through which they could create new and original concepts and ideas. They had been equipped with emotions to enable them to feel joy and sadness, achievement and despair. Emotions that allowed them to value others and to bond to them so they could appreciate and understand, both the happiness and the pain that someone else was experiencing.

The Father had also given them a will, so that they were free to consider situations and to make decisions that would influence the shape and the direction of the path they travelled through life. All these attributes were contained within the persons' soul, for this is what gave them their personality.

Perhaps the most significant aspect of human design was that the Father had created them as spiritual beings, in His own image. He Himself was Spirit and every angel was spirit. Satan understood this so well, for being a fallen angel himself, he functioned in the spirit realm. Like every angel, Satan had the ability to transform into a material body. Humans could not do that but were permanently in human form. It was the spiritual aspect of them that equipped them for eternity. Their life on earth was really but a speck in the time system into which the Father had placed them. They were created to enjoy a relationship with Him whilst living on Earth and then to spend eternity with Him in the fullness of the love and joy of His nearer presence.

Satan had chuckled gleefully and puffed out his chest with pride when he realised the full consequences of human independence from the Father. For not only had he become their god and the ruler of their world, but in breaking their relationship with the Father, humans had also forfeited their rite of passage into the fullness of the Father's Kingdom, where they would have had a place for all eternity.

The supreme Deceiver sneered at their stupidity and rolled his yellow eyes in an expression of amazement at what humans had surrendered so easily. He threw back his head and laughed hideously and then shouted aloud, ***"Now they will spend eternity with me!"***

C 9

THE BRUTALITY OF ROME

For many years demons had been busy corrupting the minds of the people of the Roman nation. They had brought to power some of the world's most politically ambitious and cruel people. People whose sanity was often in serious doubt. The desire to dominate and control others was a significant feature of their characters. Their perverted sexual desires were given free reign as power and control were established. Their leaders commanded mighty military forces and their armies were victorious. Italy's borders were expanded and other races absorbed into their sphere of influence and came under their control.

The armies of the Roman Empire were vast fighting machines that ranged far and wide. They conquered and subdued the tribes and nations around them. They were well organised and superbly lead. The Roman generals who commanded these armies were men who imposed an iron will and were able to motivate others, often using fear as one of their strongest disciplines.

The tactical planning and organisational abilities of the generals, were second to none and their military ambition and singleness of purpose, ensured they gained victory after victory.

When a victorious general returned to Rome it was customary for a huge celebration to take place and for him to lead into the city a contingent of those captured in battle. The streets were lined with Roman citizens who turned out to cheer and celebrate his victory and shout abuse at the prisoners he brought.

The victory procession, with the general on horseback at its head, followed by a large contingent of his soldiers, moved through the gates of the city and into the streets. The captives in chains, dirty, tired, hungry and afraid, were dragged along behind on their way to the slave markets or to death in the Coliseum.

To those with eyes to see and minds to understand the influence of dark spiritual forces was all too obvious. However, for the vast majority of Roman citizens, who were involved in a culture that had developed progressively and was therefore the accepted norm, this was a day of celebration.

The crowds lined the streets and cheered their victorious soldiers and called for the blood of the captives as the procession passed them. They knew that the poor defeated wretches were to be sold as slaves or were doomed to being slain by the sword of a gladiator, or eaten alive by the lions. The blood lust of Rome was aroused and in anticipation of the brutal delights that were soon to be theirs, the people shouted their vengeance upon their defeated foes.

The next few days would be a holiday and the privileged Roman citizens would enjoy the events planned for the arena of the Coliseum. They looked forward to seeing men, women and children meeting their death in the most horrible and painful ways their society could devise. Some would die slowly over several days as they hung on crosses in the streets; having been crucified. Others would meet their end more speedily as they ran to escape the claws and jaws of half-starved lions. The fighting men among them, would be given a sword and be pitted against the trained gladiators for the crowd's entertainment. Many more would be positioned around the perimeter of the arena, covered in tar and as the night events were about to commence the tar was lit and the "Roman Candles" illuminated the spectacle.

Such was their insensitivity, that the fear filled, cruel and painful death of other human beings had become entertainment for them, to be celebrated and enjoyed. Their appetite for suffering and blood seemed insatiable. They revelled in the gruesome events of dying men, women and children in the arenas and the agonisingly slow death by crucifixion.

Crucifixion was usually reserved for those guilty of the crime of sedition, actions against the State of Rome or its Emperor. It was a special way of putting enemies of the State to death and ensured that they died slowly and in the most painful way possible.

Death by crucifixion had been devised in the portals of Hell, as the result of a special meeting that had taken place between Satan and his Field Marshals. They had met in a darkened cave on the edge of a sulphurous lake, beside a steaming and active volcano and brainstormed the most cruel and painful way that a human being could have the life extinguished from them. Their minds had worked overtime as they schemed and planned until, just as dawn was breaking, the finishing touches were put to the execution method that was to become known as 'crucifixion.'

Their mouths had maliciously dripped saliva as they agreed to its format and considered what it would do to a human body; the pain and suffering that would have to be endured before the release of death finally came.

The demons had sniggered and grinned as they allowed their minds to sink to new depraved depths of vicious inventiveness. They could hardly believe how clever they had been as their evil imaginations had extended into realms not previously explored by the depraved genius of torturous thought.

As they finalised this new method of execution, Satan had authorised that it be imparted to a particular man within the hierarchy of the Roman state. He was to be allowed to receive the credit for its innovation. A high-ranking demon, skilled in mind control, was briefed and dispatched to carry out the task of implanting the concept into the mind of General Porticos Maximus.

General Maximus, was a man with all the right connections to those who held authority in the Roman senate. He was an original thinker and had shown entrepreneurial flair when he had led Roman armies and fought across the length and breadth of the Empire. He was also a cruel man with a strong sadistic streak and his treatment of those he had vanquished, had shocked even those who had fought beside him.

Now Porticos Maximus' soldiering days was over and his greying hair bore testimony to his advancing years. With his soldering career completed, the General had ambitions for political power and was cultivating those who could assist his advancement.

The confidence he had in the rightness of his previous

actions as a soldier, meant that he always slept well. A disturbed conscience was not for him, he slept soundly as a good son of Rome should and he rarely dreamed. The demon Diabloflora came to him just as the rays of dawn were touching the covers on the end of his bed.

Diabloflora entered his sleep and moved swiftly into his subconscious, implanting pictures of a man being prepared for crucifixion at the flogging post. Then the whole barbaric process unfolded before him. He saw clearly the flagellum in the legionnaire's hand, as the whip descended across the man's back opening up the skin. He heard the screams and saw the blood and gore as the whip's leather thongs, with pieces of lead and bone attached to them, tore flesh and muscle from the man's body. Then the wooden cross, the hammer and nails, the man being raised vertically on it and the absolute agony that seemingly lasted for an eternity. The final cries and gasps, as the lungs slowly filled with fluid and life slipped relentlessly away and was finally extinguished.

Porticos Maximus awoke and immediately sat bolt upright. As he relived the dream in his conscious mind, he realised that he had been given a unique opportunity to impress the upper echelons of power. Perhaps, even the Emperor himself would endorse this new means of vengeance against those who challenged Empirical authority and Rome's power.

Large portions of the Roman Empire were in a state of flux, with armies conquering new regions and more and more of the troublesome tribal areas, around its borders, being brought into submission. As influence was extended, control established and slaves taken, it was normal for the people affected by this territory-grabbing expansion to resist, retaliate and fight back. Those who led the resistance movements were to their compatriots, freedom fighters, but to the powers of Rome, they were a dangerous and seditious terrorist element. They interfered with the colonisation of neighbouring territories, the security of the Empire's borders and were to be dealt with savagely.

General Maximus did his work well. He enjoyed introducing this new method of execution and explaining its advantages, which were enthusiastically acknowledged by the senate. The Emperor had personally congratulated him and authorised its implementation. His idea, death by crucifixion, became a dreadful reality and Satan and his Field Marshals whooped and cavorted with delight.

In this climate of oppression, it was not long before those found guilty of acts of terrorism in opposition to Roman expansionism, were being sentenced to death by crucifixion. The very first was a young man, Hans, son of Ulm, who was a Hun. He had led a small band of resistance fighters to carry out a raid against the supply wagons bringing food and equipment to the Roman soldiers occupying his village. He and his men had set an ambush in a gully through which the supply wagons had to pass, but had been surprised by the number of escorting soldiers. They were seriously out numbered. The ambush failed miserably and he and four of his compatriots were captured.

Their treatment at the hands of the Roman soldiers was without mercy. They had been brutally beaten, then roped together, bound to trees and kept without food and water for several days. The local Roman commander was all for allowing his men to finish them off, but discipline was strict and his orders clear. To disobey his superiors was to place his own life at risk and so Hans and his men were assigned as prisoners of a legion returning to Rome and for the time at least, their lives were spared.

They were given the task of pulling a cart full of captured booty. It was a long and arduous journey that used up their remaining strength. Some weeks later when they arrived in Rome they were weak and emaciated with all the fight gone from them. They were imprisoned in the cells of a Roman barrack and their subsequent trial was brief and to the point. They were duly sentenced to suffer death by crucifixion.

Hans had no understanding of what crucifixion entailed, but during the days remaining to him, the prison guards delighted in leaving him in no doubt concerning the death that awaited him. They had been charged with the task of preparing the cross and ensuring that everything was ready. Hans had watched these preparations take shape and the fear inside him grew to mind numbing levels as the day of his execution approached.

He had lain all night on the damp straw in the corner of his cell, curled in the foetal position, fear numbing his mind and barely able to think. As a convicted enemy of Rome as well as a condemned prisoner, he had been given little to eat, for rations were not to be wasted on the likes of him. He should have been very hungry but food was not his focus. The stone floor on which he lay was rough and hard and stank of urine and the rats that ran around and over him should have provoked a response, but he hardly noticed any of it.

All Hans could focus on was what was about to happen to him and as the dawn began to break his body curled tighter and he began to whimper. Gone was his hatred of anything Roman. Gone was his desire to strike back against the oppressor. Gone was his courage. The demons of fear were filling his mind and exploiting his situation to the full. Finally, what he had been dreading all night happened. He heard the lock in his cell door turn and the creaking hinges groan as the door was pushed open. "Get out here, you vermin," the jailer shouted. Hans didn't move but clung to the metal ring in the wall, his knuckles showing white with the intensity of his grip. The whip in the jailer's hand came down hard and he felt it bite into his skin as intense pain penetrated his body. Rough hands grabbed and lifted him, breaking his grip, dragging him to his feet and throwing him out of the cell.

In the corridor outside, strong hands grabbed him and frog marched him into the courtyard. After the stench of the cell, the fresh air filled his lungs but was immediately expelled as a fist hit him in the solar plexus. Before he could recover, a leather thong was fastened around his wrists and passed through an iron ring above his head. Two soldiers pulled downward and he was jerked upward with his face to the whipping post and his body stretched taunt with only the tips of his toes in contact with the ground. The ends of the leather thong were secured to a second ring, lower down and he was ready for the flagellum.

With his nose against the wooden post Hans heard the centurion shout, ***"Let punishment begin!"*** The soldier standing behind him drew back his arm and he heard the swish of leather, as the flagellum was laid across his back.

The thirteen long leather strands, with pieces of lead and bone attached along their lengths, hit him and opened up his back and Hans screamed from the pain and shock. On the fourth stroke of the whip his knees gave way but the leather thong strained at his wrists and held his weight.

Again and again the whip was laid across him until his back and buttocks were nothing more than a bleeding and bloody mess. Pieces of flesh and muscle had been torn from his torso and face and he hung limp against the post, barely conscious and in more pain than he knew existed. His whole being went into shock and his heart strained to sustain his life. Hans' entire existence was reduced to the blinding, searing and all-encompassing pain that filled every part and portion of his being as the whip continued to do its work.

Time and space ceased to exist for Hans and he never heard the centurion give the orders for the whipping to stop, or for a bucket of reviving water to be thrown over him. He returned to reality as the leather thong was untied and a second lot of water hit him. He lay at the base of the wooden post, in a pool of his own blood mixed with water, a pitiful sight that now appeared barely human.

Two soldiers grabbed him under his arms and lifted him roughly to his feet. He opened his eyes and as his focus returned he saw the wooden cross lying before him. He was thrust down towards it onto the cobblestones, with the words, *"Pick it up!"* He didn't immediately understand that he was required to carry it but as he tried to catch his breath and regain his feet, fear hit him afresh with an almost physical force. He felt sick to his stomach but before he had time to react the jailer's whip struck again, this time squarely across the back of his legs. He screamed as it hit him, the force of its blow collapsing him to the ground, filling him afresh with pain and terror.

Again he was grabbed and as he staggered and cried the soldiers raised the cross and he was pushed and pulled until positioned under it. "Carry it," they shouted and released its weight onto his shoulders and pushed the cross from behind forcing him forward. His reluctant legs moved as he took his first staggering steps. He gasped as he felt the full force of the timbers and tried to balance the weight that was upon him. After a couple of steps his foot caught an uneven flagstone and he pitched forward. The cross now had a momentum of its own and it overwhelmed him. He fell under its weight, with the wood forcing him mercilessly downward, to the unyielding stones beneath him.

Again the whip in the jailer's hand spoke, striking him again across his lower legs, biting into him with a fearsome ferocity. Blood came to the surface as the skin opened up and the sandals on his feet became soaked in its redness. The air had been knocked out of his lungs and he lay gasping and bloody with his head and face being forced into the cobblestones. The pain was intense and the fear within him knew no bounds.

Suddenly the cross was lifted from him and the whip was again laid across his back. He would not have believed that such pain existed and he screamed as the nerves in his body responded to the whip's brutality. He was now almost beyond logical thought, but he knew he must get to his feet or more of the same would be dealt to him. He tried to push himself up but no longer had the strength and lay in the mud and dirt panting and crying for mercy. None came.

Hans felt a strong grip take hold of his hair and his head was jerked back, as other hands lifted him under his armpits and set him roughly on his feet. "Carry it," a voice shouted, and again he felt the weight of the cross. He started forward, and step after agonising step, he managed somehow, to stay on his feet as this procession of death made its way to the place of execution.

Slowly they moved along the roadway that led out of the city gate and down the hill. He thought the weight of the timbers would overwhelm him, but the closeness of the whip kept him focused on what he must do. Gritting his teeth he set his mind on nothing but taking the next step.

Now Hans began to notice the sound of the people around him as they taunted and jeered, shouting insults and obscenities at him. They had become a mob intent on enjoying his pain, with a blood lust that reached into the depths of inhumanity.

Suddenly they were there and he was grabbed from behind and thrown down upon the cross, that now lay in the dirt. The large rough hands of soldiers pinned his arms to the cross-member and he felt the prick of the first nail as it was positioned at his wrist. The hammer blows came without warning and he screamed as the nail was driven through the limb, grating on bone as it penetrated deep into the timber. He thrashed in pain, crying for mercy in his own language and calling for his mother.

His other arm was stretched taunt and his open hand held in place by a soldier's foot with all the man's weight ensuring it was positioned correctly to receive the second nail. His world became nothing but pain, as the soldiers continued to crucify him. With the second nail driven home they moved to his feet and in a systematic and businesslike manner they selected the next nail with care ensuring it had the length it needed to hold both his feet at a single point to the wood beneath. They crossed his ankles and drove the nail home. The pain was beyond belief as the iron nail, driven by the heavy hammer found a route through his ankles as his bowel discharged. The soldiers held their noses in mock concern at the smell, made rude remarks and laughed.

The centurion in charge watched his men work and this veteran of many long, hard and brutal campaigns, closed his eyes momentarily in acknowledgement of what he knew Hans was suffering.

The soldiers then took hold of the base of the cross and dragged it round until it was positioned at the lip of its stand. Then with several of them on either side they raised it vertically. As they did so the entire weight of Hans' body came on the three nails holding him, and the bone and tissue screamed in agony; Hans nearly fainted from the pain.

Worse was yet to come, for as he hung suspended on those three pinnacles of intense blinding pain, the base of the cross dropped into its stand and as it hit the bottom, the shock of it coming suddenly to rest, almost tore Hans from it. The pain he now experienced came from another dimension as every bone, muscle, sinew and nerve in Hans' body screamed in agony. As the weight of his entire body was taken on the nails through his wrists, the air was forced from his lungs as he hung with his arms extended. Now being suffocated by the weight of his body.

The automatic self-preservation mechanism within him,

said he must breathe and he gasped fighting for breath, but the only way he could relieve the weight on his chest was to push down against the nail through his ankles. Now as bone grated on iron a new summit of pain was experienced and Hans was shocked afresh by its magnitude and intensity. But he had to breathe, so with every breath he took, a delirious torturous agony was experienced afresh… and endured.

Satan and his Field Marshals hovered within sight and sound of all that was happening and the intensity of Hans' absolute agony, were in contrast to their satisfaction and delight.

As he hung there gasping and fighting for every breath, so thirst began to attack him. At first, Hans hardly noticed it against the agony he was experiencing throughout his body, but as time went on it set in and as he dehydrated it became another torture in itself. Desperate for water he cried out, begging for a drink, which was not given to him.

All afternoon and into the evening he hung there, a bleeding and brutal example of man's inhumanity to man. He cried, whimpered, gasped, begged and somehow endured and survived the hours of the evening and the cold of the night.

The deep biting loneliness and abandonment he experienced was borne of a realisation that he was absolutely on his own. There was no one who cared for him and no one to comfort him. His abandonment and forsakenness was complete, as crucifixion did its work in a way that no other form of execution could.

The next morning, as the first rays of dawn came into the sky and the sun began to rise, those that passed by on their way into the city beheld a pitiful sight. The blood and excrement had dried on the wood of the cross and his body retained its limp brokenness, with just enough life and strength for his breathing to continue.

There were women who pitied him and wanted to give him a drink of water, but the soldiers keeping watch over him would not allow. Their orders were clear in that regard, and anyway, their duty as executioners relieved the boredom of barrack life. Being part of an execution squad also provided them with an outlet for their resentment against an enemy, who had resisted the imperial might of which they were part. Also, they too had been forced to spend the cold night wrapped in their cloaks on the hard ground and were in no mood for sentimentality.

As the sun rose higher in the sky Hans clung to life. His mind was now focused on one thing, how to summon enough strength to breathe and thereby continue to survive. His agony continued hour after hour.

It was midafternoon when the sound of marching feet approached and the General in command of the garrison arrived at the foot of the cross with his escort of ten soldiers. The General brought military precision and colour to Hans' pain-filled existence, with his crisp uniform and glinting sword, flowing scarlet cape and plumed helmet, he made an impressive sight.

The General's escort, under the command of a Centurion, were well-drilled soldiers and moved with energy and alertness, but by now Hans was far beyond appreciating such things. The General looked at him with a detached air and spoke in a clipped military manner and with an authority that flowed from his rank, as he addressed the centurion on execution duty.

The centurion had saluted and stood stiffly to attention, listening attentively. "I need this to be ended," the General said, "there's trouble brewing in the provinces and you and your men are needed to reinforce an outlying position. Break his legs and let him die quickly and once dead, throw his body on the rubbish dump."

With his escort of soldiers closely around him, the general left knowing that an enemy's pain would now be brought to a conclusion, not out of mercy but because of strategic necessity.

The soldiers, relieved at not having to spend another night in the open and looking forward to their women and their beer, warmed to their task and got on with it immediately. They rammed the shaft of a spear under Hans' knees to act as a fulcrum and with the iron mallet with which they had driven in the nails struck his shins and broke his legs. The incredible pain momentarily revived Hans but with his legs broken he could no longer push-up to breathe and now the weight of his own body caused him to suffocate and merciful death embraced him.

In the realm of the spirit, the designers of crucifixion watched and were well pleased with their work.

C10

INCARNATION

The Father viewed all that was happening on Earth and what he saw grieved His heart. He looked upon His creation and knew that it was not as He had intended. He had created humans in His own image and given them the same basic freedoms that He has, but the way in which they were using their freedom hurt Him more deeply than He cared to admit. Their violence towards each other and their dalliance with false gods caused His heart to almost break. Yet His intense love for them was as strong as ever and He continued to love them from the very depth of His being with an everlasting love that knew no bounds.

The issue was one of freedom of will, which He had always considered essential for humans, if the relationship He wanted to have with them was to be of worth. The Father was very aware that He could have created them with an automatic desire to love, honour and worship Him and to live in peace, respect and harmony with each other. But, unless those responses came of their own motivation and choice they were of no value to Him.

Now the Father could see the terrible results of the poor choices humans had made. He had given them sovereignty over the Earth and they had surrendered it to Satan. They had in effect made this fallen angel the ruler of their world and were now subject to him, whether they realised it or not. It was the influence of the satanic that had brought death and decay to human beings and the Creation. The Father felt terribly sad, for He had made them to be eternal beings but they had opened themselves to all that was unholy and were now reaping what they had sown. Instead of love, peace and harmony they now had hatred, violence and discord, plus all the associated problems of bad relationships. Death and decay flowed naturally from the spiritual degradation of which they had chosen to be part.

The Father called to His side the most senior of His angels and spoke with Michael and Gabriel. In effect, He and they existed in a parallel dimension to the humans on Earth and although the eyes of the humans were not able to see them, they could see into the human realm with absolute clarity and were observing all that was happening.

The Father also had the capacity to hear every word spoken and to know the thoughts and desires of every heart. The situation they now observed was extreme and the Father knew that significant action was required if humans were to be salvaged from the situation of death and decay with which they had aligned themselves.

Standing with His two principal angels, they had a clear overview of all that was happening on the Earth and what they saw was appalling. They focused on the Coliseum in Rome and were saddened by the brutality and disregard for the value of human life that was so apparent. They heard the roar of the lions and the screams of those being torn to pieces and eaten alive.

They changed their focus to see what was happening around the borders of the Roman Empire and observed the destruction of a village by a troop of soldiers. They saw the rape of the women, the slaughter of the men and the houses being fired.

The trio moved on to a religious ceremony where a child was about to be sacrificed to Molak the god of war. The people were gathered in a circle around the iron god. The priest was in the process of placing a child on the out-stretched arms that would cause it to roll down and in through the opening in the gods' chest to be consumed by the fire burning in its interior.

Then their focus changed to a slave market where men, women and children were being bought and sold. The fear on the slaves' faces spoke volumes and the pain within their beings was almost unbearable. Families had been torn apart, children and parents separated. The hardness of the hearts of the perpetrators of these crimes left their consciences desensitised, untouched and unresponsive. Brutality had become the norm.

The Father's heart was sickened and the tears from the eyes of the mighty angels watching with Him were evidence of how they felt. They each knew that what they were seeing was but a brief overview, a cameo of all that was going on in the world. However, it was sufficient to allow them to know that something had to be done if the human race was not to totally self-destruct.

Since forever the Father had known what was to happen.

Now the love in His heart and the need to show them another way, in which they could behave towards Him and each other, meant that this issue was now His top priority. Speaking to the two angels He said, "This cannot be allowed to continue unchecked. They are all destined for eternal separation from me and I need to act to counter that. It is clear that they have no intention of hearing what the men I have sent to them were saying. They spoke concerning the way they are living and the morals and standards they have adopted. They must be shown another way and my Spirit imparted to those willing to receive. This is what I intend to do..."

Having heard the Father's intentions Gabriel and Michael stood with their mouths open wide in disbelief. They then tried to protest but knew that when the Father spoke, He meant what He said and that their role was to support His will and in no way to resist His intentions and actions. They bowed before their eternal Majesty and knew that they would each be called upon to perform special tasks before His rescue mission was complete.

There were a number of preparations that needed to be made before the final part of the Father's plan could be put into practice and senior angels were given important tasks to complete. The interaction between angels now took on new and awe inspired tones when they met and spoke concerning "Operation Rescue", as it came to be known. Snatches of their conversation were heard to include one of Michael's warriors saying to another, "As far as I know we'll be providing upper sector cover but we've no details yet. What's your Division going to be doing?"

Other angels, occupied by the task of selecting the right people to fill the various roles that the plan required, "What! That's a tall order. A young pure minded virgin? I'm not at all sure too many of them exist... but we'll do our best."

It was the young and inexperienced that found it hardest to comprehend what was being planned and when they met and talked, it was usually in tones that showed their lack of maturity, "He's what! Did you say, 'going down Himself'? That's incredible. They'll murder Him. I never realised He loved them that much!"

There was much to do and many arrangements to be made. The Father had made it very clear that He was laying aside His glory and power and was to become like every other human, but with one salient difference. He would not be contaminated by the historic consequences of the poor choices the humans had made. Yet, at the same time, insisted that the possibility of Him doing so whilst He was in human form, was to be very real. He was He affirmed, to become fully human and yet continue to be fully divine, although devoid of his status of Eternal Majesty.

The consternation this revelation caused among the inhabitants of Heaven was extreme. They met in small groups and expressed to each other their serious concerns. Some said, "What if his human body was attacked by disease and He became sick and died?" The angel Medicalus had stepped forward to answer that question. He said that it could not be denied that the possibility of that happening was real, but unlike humans the Father's genetic line would not contain the generational corruption that exposed so many of them to attack by disease. The risk was therefore fairly minimal. The question had been answered but the concerns continued.

A young angel, with dread written all over his countenance, said in a voice full of emotion, "It's highly dangerous down there. You've all seen what they do to each other! What if some maniac took a sword and killed Him. What then?" Nobody seemed to know the answer to that and they continued to have very real concerns.

A Statement of Proclamation was prepared and published to the angels and all other members of the Father's Kingdom to ensure that everyone understood what was being proposed. Operation Rescue was such a radical intervention in human life, that the possibility of a misunderstanding was serious. It was hoped to avoid any inappropriate intervention by an outraged heavenly being who had somehow not received all the information or perhaps had not grasped the finer points and details of the plan. The senior angels briefed their teams with care.

Finally, all the preparations had been made. The power of the Most High was to come upon a young unmarried Hebrew girl and she was to become pregnant by the power of the Holy Spirit, with the greatest gift the world was ever to receive. The archangel Gabriel was given the task of informing her that she was the Father's chosen vessel, through which He would incarnate into the world. She was at that time promised in marriage to a man. It took strong angelic influence through a dream to inform her fiancé of the circumstances of her condition and to persuade him to continue with her care and their marriage.

The Father considered the setting for His incarnation to be most important and unlike earthly kings, He wanted no pomp to accompany His arrival on Earth. He insisted on the humblest of circumstances.

From a perspective of timing, a few delays had occurred whilst the physical environment developed to the point where safety and security were not going to adversely affect the operation and the risks were acceptable. The Roman army were major players in this regard, although they had no concept or understanding of their role. The security and their occupation of the town, which had been selected as Ground Zero, was an important factor. The roads Rome had put in place would allow the rapid spread of the message and the garrisons they had established along those roads, made them comparatively safe and very useable.

The time and place was decided upon and an angelic choir rehearsed an anthem they would sing to a group of shepherds who were to be part of the proclamation process. Also a group of astral observers were to be inspired to watch the heavens for the signs that were to announce this cataclysmic event. The star these men would see had to travel from a distant galaxy and arrived just in time to play its part. They were also encouraged to bring gifts to the Incarnation that was in keeping with royal status.

The only thing left to arrange was an event that would bring all the players onto the stage at the correct moment and set everything in motion. The Heavenly committee set up to oversee Operation Rescue finally decided that a Roman census would be just the thing to do this. Proclamatus, a senior angel, was sent to speak into the mind of the Roman ruler, Emperor Augustus to set that in motion.

The rules by which the census was to operate required that everyone return to the town in which their father had been born and large numbers of people began to migrate to comply with this directive. The Chosen Vessel and the man to whom she was betrothed made their journey and it was at this time, that the Incarnation occurred and she gave birth to the Godchild.

In the realm of the spirit, Satan was ruling supreme upon the Earth and was delighted in the way his influence was spreading. He and his demons celebrated in the most hideous ways each time their temptation and corruption of people resulted in human society descending to a new level of degradation. His demons ranged far and wide across the Earth with apparent impunity. They had become so acceptable to humans that they were welcomed either overtly or covertly but received and accepted none the less.

It was a local demon commander in the Middle East, that first realised something was afoot. One of his junior demons was on a routine patrol around the region when he overheard a conversation between one of the astronomers and a local inhabitant. The astronomer was trying to discover the exact place in which the Incarnation was going to occur. This snatch of conversation was reported back and the commander, who, realising the importance of the information, took it straight to Satan himself believing that by doing so he would be able to curry favour with his Master.

General Decepticus, waited in an anteroom for an audience

with his Commander in Chief and felt deep inside him the anxiety that was always present when any of them spoke directly to him. With his helmet under his arm and his sword in its scabbard, he was escorted into Satan's presence between two members of Satan's personal bodyguard. They were absolute brutes, at least half as big again as the General and with an obvious devotion to their Master that precluded any possibility of assassination even being contemplated.

They never moved from Decepticus' side and their contained aggression, reminded him of guard dogs on a chain who could be unleashed at any moment. Their pungent smell, extended claws and dripping fangs encouraged him to have the right attitude of servility before his Lord Satan. Although he outranked his escort significantly, he knew instinctively there was only one being whose orders they obeyed and that was not him.

The heavy metal portcullis barring the entrance to Satan's inner sanctum rose in front of them as a demon who was part of the Security Corps turned the capstan allowing the trio to pass through the entrance. As he moved beneath the heavy iron barrier into the semi-darkness within, it took a moment or two for General Decepticus' eyes to adjust to the twilight world of his Master. He felt the tension and oppression within his body as the muscles of his chest tightened with the fear that had started to grip him. He was determined to remain outwardly calm and confident, but at a deeper level he was already wondering if he had been wise to ask for an audience with the most cunning, depraved and vicious power in the universe.

The sulphurous ash under his feet crunched and the sound alerted "guard dogs" of hideous proportions, that growled savagely and launched themselves at him, as he passed each one. Their restraining chains, secured to the collars around their necks, were long enough for them to attack and just short enough to prevent them reaching him. The hair on the back of his neck stood on end and his right hand wanted to move instinctively to the hilt of his sword. However, he knew he must not show either fear or aggression and continued to march with an enormous demon on either side of him. The air about him was filled with a cloud of tiny twittering and hissing demons that flew just above his head and heralded his approach.

As he moved deeper into the cavern General Decepticus became aware of something happening deep within the cave's corners on his left and right. As his yellow eyes became accustomed to the gloom he could just make out what it was and the pain filled sounds coming to him helped him identify their source.

He realised that in one corner was a demon secured to a metal ring in the cave's roof, in such a way, that he was stretched taunt with just the tips of his toes in contact with the ground. Behind him a fire in a brazier was glowing red-hot and the demon was being slowly cooked alive. The miserable wretch was just able to turn slowly around like meat being roasted on spit. His agonising cries and pleas for mercy were pitiful to hear.

In the cave's opposite corner were a vastly different scene, but the sounds coming from it told the General that another form of torture was taking place. There appeared to be a large metal case, the outline of which was an oversized body standing upright with its two halves hinged and partially open. General Decepticus had heard about this form of torture which was known as the Iron Maiden and could see, that inside was a demon with the tips of large sharp iron spikes penetrating all parts of his body. He could see dark green blood oozing from around each spike. As he watched a gruesomely grotesque demon-torturer turned a handle on the side of the case that caused it to close a little more. The screams this induced from the demon inside were terrifying and blood curdling.

Satan stood in the gloom at the back of the cave and was practically invisible as he blended with the darkened background. A sneer played around the corners of his mouth as he watched the General being marched towards him. When Decepticus was still some ten metres away, he released the cloak that covered him and as it fell to the floor and he became instantly visible. The shocked look on the General's face told Satan, he had achieved maximum impact and Decepticus fell to his knees, before his Master with his forehead almost in contact with the ground. Satan lowered himself onto the throne that was positioned just behind him and having adopted a regal pose felt, that he could afford to be civil. He spoke with a convivial tone in his voice, "What can I do for you General Decepticus? I'm pleased to see you looking so well. You may kiss my feet and then rise and make your report."

Decepticus did as he was bid and then raised his head from its bowed position and stood to his feet. His metal-edged, leather armour creaked and clanked a little as he did so, and the sword at his side swung again to its position of balance. He was careful not to engage those red eyes that looked upon him with obvious distain and he wasn't fooled by Satan's friendly words, but focused on a point in the middle distance over Satan's shoulder. "I thank you my Lord for agreeing to see me," he began, "I bring information that I believe you would want to hear immediately for it concerns a most serious matter."

He was interrupted by a growl that struck him in the pit of his stomach and awakened the fear that never slept for long. "Get on with it," the growl said, "I haven't all day to listen to your ramblings." The blade of fear twisted inside him, his stomach knotted afresh and he knew the ground upon which he stood was indeed fragile.

He took a deep breath and began again, "I have evidence that strongly suggests that the Father is planning to incarnate into His creation as a human being, a boy child I believe. I came to you personally My Lord, because I felt this was information that should not be entrusted to the normal intelligence network and that you would want to hear it directly." Decepticus paused for effect and took a deep breath. Before he could say anything more, Satan spoke, "Incarnation, you say! And where and when is this unlikely event to take place, General!" The words and the tone with which they were spoken said to General Decepticus that he had better have some answers or he would pay a heavy price for any misinformation or ignorance. His body stiffened involuntarily as he began, "My Lord, as far as I have been able to establish it may have already happened, or will occur very soon. The place being mentioned seems to be a small town in the province of Judea, called Bethlehem and that My Lord, concludes my report."

Satan fixed the general with a stare that would have not been out done by a laser beam and said, "No! You have not finished General, because you have not told me the reason for this so called 'INCARNATION,' what do you say is its purpose?"

The General knew with every part of his being that he had made a tactical error in coming personally to Satan and fleetingly wished he had sent an underling to be vapourised by those eyes and this intense cross examination. His right claw like hand tightened around the scabbard that held his sword and feeling the confidence that it gave him, he began to speak, "It would seem my Lord, that the Father, fool that He is, wishes to draw the men and women of the human race back into relationship with Himself. It is something I cannot pretend to understand fully but He seems to want to relate to them and cannot whilst their actions and behaviour are as they are."

Satan rose from the throne on which he had been sitting and took two paces towards the General, who proven warrior that he was, felt he wanted to turn and run, but knew to do so would prove fatal. His stomach turned to ice but he held his ground and waited for whatever was about to befall him.

Satan stopped with his massive head just inches from Decepticus' face and the General was treated to the full force of the sulphurous stench of his breath. He began quietly, "Are you telling me, General, that you believe all the filth and corruption I have put in place, all the destruction and death that I have so cleverly orchestrated, all the temptations and deceptions that have proved so effective are about to be undone?" Then he screamed, "Rubbish!! Poppycock!! You're a fool and an incompetent imbecile to think that I don't know what is being planned and am not one step ahead of Him!"

Satan paused for effect, opened his jaws as if to bite off Decepticus' head and the General glimpsed the green slime of his saliva and the black staining on his teeth. The foulness of his breath caused the General to stop breathing momentarily and he knew he dared not flinch or reveal the fear that held him in its icy grip. The giant mouth closed and the growl was again sounding in his ear, "Get out of here General, before you find yourself in one of my dungeons and be careful not to waste my time again." Decepticus bowed and turned and with the brutes still on either side of him, marched crisply out, with unspoken relief at having escaped with his life, filling every part of him.

Satan pondered what General Decepticus had told him and made a mental note to have the spies, who should have picked up this information, tortured and put to death. He cast his mind around the problem, knowing that he risked the destruction of all he had worked so hard to establish on the Earth, if he could not eliminate the Godchild. He knew the region that Decepticus had mentioned and wondered which of his satanic agents it would be best to work through. He wanted to choose someone who actually had the authority to fix the problem once and for all and leave no loose ends.

He ground his teeth in anger at the very thought of his work being undone. He had made such splendid progress and his influence was so well established, that he felt sure this desperate measure that the Father was initiating, could easily be undone and the Godchild snuffed out. One of his best agents was the man he had appointed king of that land, he sneered venomously, at the thought of the satisfaction and enjoyment Herod would get from what he had in mind. He called into his presence his Chief of Staff and watched the leer on Field Marshal Sadisticus' face grow from ear to ear as he briefed him on this special assignment.

Sadisticus loved his work and the more evil and sadistic his assignments, the more his insatiable bloodlust was invigorated and stimulated. He felt the euphoria within, that came every time he was given the task of arranging the death of a child. Now, his anticipated pleasure was heightened to a new pinnacle of gratification at the thought of all the baby boys in the region being put to the sword. His mind was turning summersaults of delight as he left to implement his master's commands.

He found Herod in a bedroom of his palace, inflicting indescribable sexual acts upon a young boy. As he watched, he knew that the success of his assignment was assured. Herod was definitely the man for this job and as Sadisticus watched, Herod collapsed onto the bed panting and satisfied from his perverted activity. Field Marshall Sadisticus entered his mind and began the process of implanting the thoughts that were to bring death to a generation of baby boys and the wailing and gnashing of teeth to their mothers. Field Marshal Sadisticus knew he had to be successful and as Herod dozed he remained longer than usual and penetrated deep into the man's subconscious mind.

The angels who comprised the Incarnation Preparation Organisation, had been busy for some time with the arrangements for which they were responsible. It was one of their number, Bravarius, who had just finished his shift as part of the Chosen Vessel's Protection Squad, when he felt the presence of the demonic deep in his spirit. It was like radar picking up an enemy fighter and as he tuned his discernment more finely, the alarm bells went off in his head as he realised what he was receiving.

Bravarius had fought many demons, but the evil his discernment was now detecting was almost off the scale. It caused him to feel somewhat nauseous as he contemplated its seriousness and its magnitude. The information he was receiving loud and clear in his spirit was Sadisticus' speaking to Herod and he was shocked to realise the implications of the plot he had uncovered.

The chairman of the Incarnation Preparation Committee was a magnificent angel, of very senior rank named Centauries and it was to him that the warrior, Baravarius went at such speed that he left a trail of silver light in his wake. The urgency that Bravarius felt meant that he bypassed the normal protocol of going through his Divisional Commander and went directly to the senior angel he knew had the authority and wisdom to deal with the situation.

As Bravarius explained the discernment he had received in his spirit, the great angel immediately understood the critical implications of what he was being told. The corrupt and malignant character of Herod was well known and his ruthlessness an established fact. Centauries knew that he had to act swiftly if disaster was to be averted.

There was no time to brief and dispatch one of the messenger angels, normally assigned to this kind of task, for the sake of expediency Centauries undertook the task himself. As a member of the Incarnation Preparation Committee he knew exactly where the Chosen Vessel, her new husband and the

Incarnation, were staying and with his blazing sword drawn he hurtled silently across the distance separating him from them.

As Centauries approached the trio he was greatly relieved to find that that he was not too late. He could only just make out the ring of angels from the Protection Squad in position around their location, guarding them in the spiritual realm from demonic attack. If he had not known they were there he would never have penetrated their camouflage. He quickly made his presence known, found the Commanding Officer and informed him of his mission. The small family was sleeping peacefully and he immediately entered the man's slumber and gently spoke to him through a dream.

The message that Centauries conveyed was simple, yet critical. It was to inform the man that Herod would be looking for the child in order to kill him. To prevent that from happening he was to immediately take the Chosen Vessel and the Incarnation to an adjacent land. Centauries also said that he would inform the man when it was safe for them to return.

The final thing that Centauries did was to make sure the man was fully awake and preparing to leave. Their departure occurred within the hour. With great stealth they made their way across the border and away from Herod's evil intentions.

The dream Herod had that night was both graphic and horrific and Field Marshal Sadisticus left out none of the details. When Herod awoke, it was with a purpose clear in his mind and he quickly instructed the centurion in charge of the garrison to assemble his men and go and kill every baby boy under the age of two years that lived in the town.

When the town's resident demons became aware of what

was to happen, they whooped and yelled and celebrated with a sadistic delight that came straight from the depths of their depravity. To ensure the killing happened and that there were to be no softening of the soldiers resolve, Field Marshal Sadisticus ordered that every soldier involved be motivated by a demon of bloodlust who would indwell them and encourage them in their task.

At first light the soldiers were assembled and given their orders. The demons were also there and entered the minds of them all. As they marched crisply from the garrison the desire to kill was strong in each one.

The next three hours were horrific for the families living in the small town as homes were forcibly entered and children slaughtered. The soldiers, with an enthusiasm that was demonically inspired, put every baby boy to death. Throats were cut, or swords thrust through the small bodies.

Many a parent attempted to protect their children and received the soldiers' wrath. Mothers were beaten aside whilst men were brutally subdued with an iron clad fist, dagger or sword. The soldiers worked in pairs moving from house to house and street-to-street leaving in their wake a trail of blood, death and grief. The town hardly knew what had hit it and by the time the soldiers had finished, a generation of baby boys no longer existed.

Herod received a report from the Commanding Officer of the garrison, informing him that his orders had been carried out, whilst Sadisticus reported the success of the venture directly to Satan. All were well pleased.

C11

THE TESTING

Time passed and some years later, the angel Centauries, again visited the man in a dream informing him of Herod's death and that it was safe for them to return to their own country. Herod, the Roman puppet king, had died in a most horrible way. He had spent his life as a satanic agent and when Satan had finished with him, worms consumed him from the inside of his body.

The Godchild grew physically, in wisdom and in spiritual stature. During those developmental years, Michael's warrior angels had acted as His bodyguards and had on a number of occasion's battled and repelled demons to keep the Incarnation safe. Yet it was His own righteousness, purity and devotion to the will of the Father that was always His first line of defense.

Satan had long been aware that his murderous attempt to kill the Incarnation during Herod's reign had failed. Now the Great Tempter, was ready to try a different approach in an attempt to neutralise the Incarnation's mission and to turn the situation to his own advantage.

Very aware that the Incarnation was God, in human form, Satan also understood that in becoming a man He had laid aside His glory and was functioning out of his humanity. It was His humanity that Satan decided to target. He was conscious of the moral frailness of human beings and the desire for wealth and power that is potentially in the heart of everyone. For he placed it there? Had not he been absolutely victorious in driving the wedge of independence between human beings and the Father? Had not he been successful in becoming the ruler of the world? Did not almost every human being bow the knee to his sovereignty and Lordship?

He felt certain that if the temptations he was able to offer were juicy enough, no human being would be able to resist and the Incarnation was fully human. Satan looked heavenward and shouted a defiant, "Yes," as affirmation of the victory he felt certain would be his.

The new day had dawned quietly enough with strong sunlight breaking through the clouds and warming the land. The wind had died away the night before and was now no more than a gentle breeze. The sky above was as blue as could be and the ground beneath solid to the tread of many feet.

The man they called The Baptiser, would be busy again with many coming to him seeking a new start in their relationship with the God of their forefathers; whom they worshipped in their temple and honoured on their feast days.

Those that came for baptism wanted to be rid of the corruption in their spirit and in their life. Satan, the Tempter, hated this man with a vengeance. He had used every means he had to corrupt him, but the purity of his life and the conviction inherent in his preaching of repentance, gave no ground. Satan swore the foulest oath he could muster, growled and ground his teeth whilst plotting the man's destruction. He reasoned that if he could not tempt and corrupt him he would silence him some other way and began to consider how he might do it.

The sunlight glinted on the water in which the Baptiser stood waist deep. The power in the words he had spoken had done its work, as was borne witness by the constant stream of repentant souls coming to him for baptism. Suddenly, the Baptiser's spirit danced with delight as Purity and Truth came closer and closer to him, until he was standing face to face with the Incarnation. He felt the strong urge to kneel before Him; this human manifestation of God and it was only the depth of water that denied him the privilege and prevented him from doing so.

When he realised what was expected of him, the Baptiser protested, but at the Incarnation's insistence he carried out what he considered to be a totally unnecessary baptism of repentance. As he finished, the Holy Spirit descended and filled the Incarnation with His power and Presence. The Baptiser looked on in awe and wonderment.

The Great Dragon was also there, but hid himself well and looked on from a distance. The upper atmosphere was so full of angelic beings that he was most careful not to expose himself to their swords which blazed and flashed crimson and gold in the hands of the mighty angelic warriors under Michael's command.

The Holy Spirit now became the leading player in a drama that was rapidly gathering momentum, as He drove the

Incarnation out into the desert away from all visible means of support. Satan saw Him go and followed clandestinely. Gone were family and friends, gone were the angels. All that was left was a man, the desert and the Tempter following closely and silently on His heels.

The sun rose higher in the sky as the journey continued into the heat and desolation of that barren place. There the Incarnation remained day after day, until forty dawns had broken and forty sunsets had disappeared over the horizon. The needs the Incarnation had as a human, came to the fore. He had not eaten for all this time and His body was weakened. Now was the moment of opportunity and Satan spoke his guile into His being. The hoary old Devil reached deep into his great depth of deceit and cunning and pulled out all the stops. Satan knew that this was the moment of truth and that he might never again encounter the Incarnation in such a weakened physical state, that he must press home his advantage.

The pride that buoyed Satan up had produced a serious delusion. In a very real sense he was completely misguided in his belief, that he had the same status as the Incarnation and that he could rightly challenge for the leadership of the Father's Kingdom. Reality said it was no contest, but to have the Incarnation in physical form and with his glory laid aside, gave him the best possible chance of success and he was going to give this opportunity everything he had.

The Incarnation knew deep in his psyche that He was the physical manifestation of the Living God, that all the power of the universe was at his disposal. Basically, He could do anything He wanted for He had infinite power at his disposal.

He did not need to remain hungry for the Incarnation could create food from anything. He was aware that He only had to desire their help and angels would be there to do His bidding, to protect Him and to ensure His safety. The kingdoms of the world were there for Him to command and rule if He so chose. But He also knew that to succumb to temptation and misuse His power, would put him outside the Father's perfect will. So the issue became one of obedience. Would He give in to his hunger, to greed, to worldly possessions and to the misuse of power or would He remain faithful to His commission and stand fast against everything the Tempter offered Him?

Satan sensed that it was probably now or never. With boldness borne of ambition and an insatiable desire to rule the Father's Kingdom he spoke directly to the Incarnation and tempted Him. Satan offered solutions to all the issues confronting Him.

The Devil was prepared to give everything that was within his power to give, to pollute the Incarnation's sinless character. To bring Him down to the fallen level of all other humans and so destroy the Godhead and The Mission. The Kingdom would then be his!

In His humanity the Incarnation desired the things that Satan was offering but the strong resolve that under girded the very fabric of His being was towards obeying the will of the Father.

Heaven was hushed and had virtually come to a standstill as every angel and heavenly being waited for the outcome of the contest that was being played out on the stage of the Earth. It was as if Heaven held its breath, for they all understood the significance of what was occurring. If the Incarnation, in his Holy Spirit filled humanity, was able to defeat the Evil One by not succumbing to temptation, then so could any human being similarly equipped.

Finally, the two stood face to face as Satan made his bid for sovereignty. He was prepared to give the world and everything the world contained to the Incarnation, in exchange for the Incarnation's submission to him and worship of him.

The Incarnation's rejection was both immediate and definite and it was as if there had never really been a contest at all. Every being in Heaven breathed a huge sigh of relief and a group of angels went to assist Him.

C12

THE MISSION

The power of evil had dominated the minds and controlled the actions of human beings for so long, that the Incarnation's presence among them, stood in stark contrast to the spiritual darkness to which they were accustomed. In the realm of the spirit the forces of darkness held sway and as the Incarnation moved through that darkness a reaction to His presence took place. Demons had taken up residence within many people bringing sickness, infirmity or insanity to the people they inhabited. They were most reluctant to leave their host's body but had no answer to the spiritual authority of the Incarnation.

On one occasion a young demon by the name of Silentus, was really enjoying causing a man to be dumb. The man concerned was suffering terribly and since Silentus had taken up residence within him and attached himself to his vocal chords, he had not been able to utter a word. Doctors had prescribed all manner of remedies and the man had swallowed any number of pills and potions, but Silentus had simply laughed at their ineffectiveness and tightened his grip. He knew that spiritual problems required a spiritual solution and they were trying to solve this one with a medical remedy. He wound his talons tighter and bounced up and down in glee causing the man to shake and hold his throat.

Suddenly, the spiritual atmosphere around Silentus changed and he sensed the difference immediately. No longer was he feeling comfortable and cocky but had started to feel decidedly nauseous. His pallor changed from his normal bright orange to a sickly green and then a dirty yellow and he felt very unwell. The reason for his distress was the Incarnation, who was now standing directly in front of the man and as He opened his mouth to speak, Silentus knew exactly what was coming.

The words of command the Incarnation spoke carried an authority that no demon could withstand and Silentus was no exception. On being told to leave, Silentus could do nothing but release his grip on the man's vocal cords and prepare to depart. Actually, he was pleased to go for he would have done anything to get away from the Incarnation and the powerful spiritual forces of love and concern that He emitted. Forces, that carried the very essence of holiness and purity and Silentus hated to be anywhere near such influences. As the man opened his mouth, Silentus escaped through it and as he speedily departed he heard the man begin to speak.

The people saw the Incarnation's power and He quickly became a super star. People flocked to Him wherever He went, bringing their sick and demon possessed and He drove out the demons and healed the sick. He also taught the people many things concerning the Father's love for them and showed them how the Kingdom of Heaven was close to them and how they could be part of it.

One person whose life was dramatically changed was a man who had an eye disease that had caused him to go blind and this is his story.

"I was very hungry! I'd begged all yesterday and received nothing and as the sun got hot around midday I tried to stay in the shade, away from the worst of its heat. My head ached and I felt faint, but knew I had to stay on my feet and continue calling out or I would be completely ignored. I wondered how much longer I could keep going without food, so I summoned my remaining strength and carried on begging. I cursed my eyes for not working and wondered for the ten thousandth time why I had gone blind.

Fortunately there was still a little water in the leather skin that hung from my waist and from time to time, I sipped its contents and hoped I'd be able to find more when it ran out. The rags that covered me I knew, were filthy for they had been other people's cast offs when I got them and I had worn them unwashed for years. Even I knew how bad I smelt, but my priority was to try to get enough food each day to stay alive and I had neither time nor energy to worry about niceties. My life had always been one of day-to- day survival and I never ever got enough to eat.

Sometimes the boys from the village ragged me or threw stones at me and even stole the little I did have. Life was always hard and there were times when I thought I'd be better off dead, but somehow I carried on, always hoping that things would improve but they never did!

I had heard that there was a teacher in the land who had healed a paralytic by the power of his word. I didn't really believe that stuff, because after all, seeing is believing and I couldn't see, could I? But let me tell you what happened next.

I was in the market begging as usual and I'd just been given a piece of really stale bread, on which I had dripped some water trying to soften it. I heard the people around me get noisy and excited and a real hubbub began. I could feel the village folk pressing all around me and I asked Simon, the leather worker beside whose stall I was sitting, what was going on. He ignored me at first so I grabbed his arm and asked again. He told me the Teacher was coming with some of his men. I could hear the noise getting closer so I decided to give it a go, after all what had I got to lose?

I started to shout out and they all told me to be quiet, but I didn't care what they thought. So I just carried on shouting at the top of my voice asking him to have mercy on me. People said, "Belt up," and "Shhhhh," but I mustered everything I had and really let rip and was bellowing for all I was worth.

The next thing I knew, Simon was grabbing me and telling me to get up because the Teacher was calling to me. This was my big chance and as Simon steered me in his direction, I headed for the centre of the noise. It felt really nice as I got close to Him and I just knew that what I'd heard about the paralytic was true. He had a real nice voice and he asked me what I wanted him to do. Now, as we know I'm blind and I have to say I thought the answer to that question would have been obvious, but I know how to be respectful so I just said I wanted to see again and do you know, the next thing was, I could!

I could see the Teacher with his beard and white robe and his men around him, all the people in a large group. I looked up and saw the blue sky with white clouds. I'd forgotten what colour was like and its impact was fantastic. I looked around and saw the village people. Then the full impact of what he had done hit me and I could not contain what I felt any longer. I whooped and yelled and grabbed him and kissed his feet. I could not thank him enough for healing me, I was blind but now I could see. Amazing!

My life has really changed since that day. Simon said that if I washed and got rid of the smell, he'd let me help on his stall and when that worked out, he showed me how to make things out of leather. He says my work isn't bad and is starting to sell. But the very first thing I did was to go and find my sister, show her my new eyes and tell her that I can see. She could hardly believe it but couldn't deny what had happened to me."

Not everyone who came into contact with the Incarnation was happy about it.

They met early in the morning, straight after breakfast, to consider what they should do. The two men were partners in an undertaking business and they were most unhappy. The funeral that they had gone to a lot of trouble and expense to arrange yesterday, had been a shambles. They had never seen anything like it and they certainly did not want a repeat performance. They settled back into their seats and looked at each other, not quite knowing how to begin. Then Jahaza lent forward towards Simeon and in a doleful tone said, "What are we going to do about this, he can't be allowed to get away with it and its cost us money we need to get back?"

Tugging at his beard as he always did when worried Simeon looked down at his feet and replied to his friend, "What worries me, is that if he continues raising people from the dead we'll end up not having a business and we'll go broke. It's all very well for the widow having her son alive again, but what about us, how are we supposed to earn a living with people like him around? Do you think we could get the Sanhedrin to ban him from doing this stuff, would they be interested in helping us?"

From what his friend was saying, Jahaza saw some light at the end of his dark tunnel. Stifling a yawn, for he'd slept very badly last night worrying about the business, tossing and turning and trying not to keep his wife awake. The last thing he needed was to upset her on top of everything else, but with some hope in his voice he said, "Do you think the Council would do that, I suppose it's worth a try. We could talk to Beraiah and see if he would support us and take our case to the elders. Let's go round and see if he's in."

He made to get up but relaxed down again as Jahaza spoke, "That's okay and we must do that, but what about the money we're out of pocket. The widow didn't seem interested in paying us when I spoke to her, but she always was as tight as a drum where money was concerned. She was away with the fairies after it happened, hugging and kissing the boy and crying all over the place and then hugging and kissing everyone in sight, she even tried to hug me. She might have settled down a bit by now and be willing to pay part of the cost for the bit of the funeral we did have. Those spices and the frankincense cost us plenty."

It was Simeon who suddenly realised that it was worse than he had first thought, as he remembered the gravediggers and the mourners they'd hired and he groaned as he thought of them wanting their money. Jahaza heard him groan and looked questioningly at his friend, raising an eyebrow, by way of asking what the problem was, "The gravediggers and mourners will want paying too. That'll take all our spare cash, but we will have to pay them or we won't get them again." A deeper mood of melancholy settled on the pair as they got up to go and find Beraiah.

Meanwhile, with great stealth, Satan observed what was happening and hated the Incarnation and every action He took to undo what he had put in place. Yet, he still had his victories and chuckled with demonic glee every time he recalled how he had dealt with the Incarnation's appointed forerunner. He delighted in bringing to mind the executioner's sword slicing off his head and the Baptiser's lifeless body slumping to the floor. "Repentance!" he shouted out loud, "that's how I deal with those that preach repentance." He saw in his mind's eye the girl dancing and Herod's infatuation and revelled afresh in how easy it had all been. He felt sure that all he would have to do is to be patient and he would be able to deal with the Incarnation in a similar manner.

The life of a young boy was seriously affected by his encounter with the Incarnation and this is his story.

"We all got up very early and I had a hard job getting out of bed. My mother lit two candles for us to dress by and we ate breakfast in their yellow glow, then left whilst it was still dark outside. The first rays of the sun crept over the hills and into the village as we made our way along the track that would take us to where we hoped the Healer would be.

We had heard from the man who came running and shouting last night about how He could heal people. All the adults had met and decided to go today to where He was. Nearly everyone in our village was up and walking and we had with us, all the sick and those who had gone strange in the head.

I was helping Uncle Josh along, who leaned on me because of his leg that wouldn't support his weight properly. He'd hit it with an axe whilst chopping wood and broken the bone and now used a crutch on one side of him and me on the other. The leg was really quite a mess and I didn't like looking at it, because it made me feel a bit sick. I really hoped he would get his leg healed today because he was so heavy and it would be a long way home with his weight on me.

Three other people were on stretchers and the men carrying them, took it in turns to hold the handles, because they got heavy after a while and it was hard work getting them up the hills and down through the gullies.

It was nearly mid-morning before we got there and I had never seen such a big crowd before in my life. I didn't know there were that many people in the world. Everyone was so excited because of what was happening. He had already healed a lot of people and there were people jumping about, shouting and crying that He'd fixed their backs or their arm or whatever had been wrong or hadn't worked before. There was a whole group of men and women who were lepers and he had healed them and they were kicking up a dreadful din, singing and crying, thanking Him and carrying on. We made our way through the crowd and what a noise they were making, I was so excited, it was better than any of the festivals I'd been to.

His men had formed a circle around Him and only allowed

people through a couple at a time, but we got close enough to see what He was doing. A man who was paralysed and lying on a bed was brought and put in front of Him; He just put His hands on him and I heard Him tell the man to get up and straight away the man did. At first the man just stood looking at Him and then he moved his body from side to side and then his arms in big circles and then he walked forward and let out a tremendous yell and started to run around shouting and yelling, that he had been healed after not being able to move for fifteen years. It was amazing stuff.

During the afternoon more people arrived from the villages further away and my mum and dad met relatives I'd never seen before but had only heard about. The whole hillside was full of people who were so excited about what was happening, because all the sick were getting healed.

I helped my Uncle Josh move to where the Healer was, in the middle of all the people and we had to wait quite a while before his turn came. I was allowed to help him forward and then stand beside him. I heard the Healer ask him what he wanted Him to do. My uncle Josh started to cry and could hardly speak. He pointed to his leg and just managed to say that he wanted it healed. The Healer put his hands on my uncle's leg and for a second or two nothing happened, then there was a loud crack and I saw his shinbone move and the leg straighten.

My uncle Josh let out a loud cry, as he saw the skin around the damaged leg move and there was a loud cracking noise as the bone came back into alignment. All the damage disappeared and suddenly his leg was well again. Uncle Josh nearly fell over, he was so surprised and he leaned on me real heavy. Then he straightened up and dropped the crutch he'd been using and let out a yell like I'd never heard before, jumped up and down and danced around for all he was worth. I looked at the Healer and He smiled then moved on to the next person, a women who was blind.

The day was very exciting and I could hardly believe the things I saw happen as the Healer did his work. I was fascinated by the way He dealt with those who were not in their right mind, or who had demons inside of them. He just spoke and commanded the evil spirits to leave and they did! Some of them made the person shake all over and others let out real loud shouts and screams but they all came out when he told them to.

It was really interesting and I watched for a long time. I hardly noticed the light beginning to fade. Then I heard his men talking to Him, saying how late it was getting and shouldn't the people be sent away to find food. A little while later one of them asked if anyone had any food left and nobody did, except me that is. I still had the barley loaves and fishes my mum had given me for my lunch, which I hadn't eaten because I'd not thought of food all day and it was only now that food was being talked about, that I realised how hungry I was. I got them out and was about to eat them, when one of his men took them from me and took my lunch to the Healer.

I knew something was going to happen because they were making everyone sit down on the grass, but I didn't know what. I stayed as close to the Healer as I could and I saw Him look upward into the sky and heard Him give thanks for the food.

Then He broke my lunch into pieces and gave the bits to his men and they gave it to the people.

I was sure it wasn't going to go very far because it wasn't a very big lunch, but the most amazing thing happened. The more his men gave to the people, the more there seemed to be and half an hour later, when it was getting really quite dark, people were still being given bits of my lunch and everyone had plenty to eat.

When all the people were satisfied the Healer had all the scraps collected up. I helped gather them and there was much more left over than my original lunch. I don't know how He did it but then I don't know how He was able to heal my uncle Josh and all the other sick people either, but he did."

The Incarnation was having a very positive effect on the lives of many people, but there were those who resisted His influence because the light that He emitted clashed with the darkness within them. One such person was Bethuel, the leader of the local synagogue and the 'clash of kingdoms' that occurred in his spirit, was to have far reaching consequences.

Some of us had a meeting last night over what happened last Saturday in the synagogue, because none of us had ever seen anything like it. Caleb should not have been there of course, because as you know the sick or lame or imperfect are not normally allowed into the synagogue, but we had told him to be there, even though his hand was paralysed and his arm withered. We had heard that the Nazarene was a Sabbath breaker and set things up so that we would have proof, if he did have the audacity to heal on the Lord's Day, the day when no one is allowed work.

I got there early as I normally do, to open the doors and get everything ready. A dozen or so people had arrived when he came in. We had primed Joshua to ask the all-important question about whether it was legal to heal on the Sabbath. It was a bit pointed perhaps, but at least he would know what the issue was and if he then went ahead and healed Caleb it would be in defiance of what he knew was lawful.

Well, it all went precisely as we had planned. Joshua spoke to him and put the question to him and this self-appointed Teacher prattled on about, "What if a sheep fell into a deep hole, would the owner not lift it out on the Sabbath?" Well of course you would but he didn't seem to understand that we are not talking about sheep, but about healing a man and that is quite different, isn't it?

Anyway he fell into the trap good and proper because not only did he understand the issue but straight away told Caleb to stretch out his arm and as he did so, the Sabbath law was broken because his hand was healed and became just like his other one. To do that kind of work on the Sabbath is a real 'no no' and he knew it.

I spoke to Caleb afterwards when everyone else had gone. I told him he should not have carried on like he did, thanking him, kissing his feet and saying how he would now be able to earn a proper living again, to feed his family real food instead of them eating scraps. I gave him a real tongue lashing because that kind of talk only encourages the lawbreakers to keep on breaking the law and that's the last thing we want.

Well, as I was saying, this is a very serious issue and the meeting agreed something definite needed to be done. We can't have everyone thinking the Sabbath Laws don't mean anything and that they can do what they like on the Sabbath, well they can't!

This man has to be stopped. A lot of people are starting to listen to his homespun philosophies; it is the Pharisees that interpret the Law and say what goes, not some uneducated carpenter from some place out in the sticks. Imagine if we allowed every self-appointed, wandering, upstart to challenge and change the traditions of the elders. Why, the whole religious system we keep in place would be vulnerable and what would happen then to our position and privileges? Anyway, I'm pleased to say that the meeting saw the sense of what was being said and made the decision to do away with this impostor. The details of how he will be killed are yet to be decided, but in principle we have their agreement to move towards ensuring his permanent removal. Good riddance to bad rubbish I say!"

In the unseen realm of the spirit, the demon Antichristos, drew his black wings about him and laughed sadistically at how easy it had been to manipulate the thinking of a man; who was all puffed up with pride and was guarding his privileges. He hoped for some reward for doing such a good job. Perhaps he would be allowed to torment the Incarnation when the death sentence was carried out.

C13
BETRAYAL

Palestine had so much demonic activity going on within its borders that it had become a strong satanic principality. Demonic powers held sway in the lives of most of the people. Even so the Incarnation was causing a shift in emphasis to occur as the people were healed physically and demons were cast out.

The religious leaders were challenged by what they saw happening. Some realised that the Father was at work among them as the power of His kingdom flowed from the Incarnation, changing lives and setting people free. Others refused to accept that there was a spiritual authority greater than the gods they worshipped and resisted all that the Incarnation was doing. They worked against this revelation of the Father's love because their position, authority and status were at stake.

In the realm of the spirit, the demons were busy influencing the priests and Pharisees. They were working overtime to ensure that their plans for the Incarnation's destruction were moving towards a definite conclusion.

The religious leaders had so much pride and such a strong desire to retain their positions of privilege and power, they had succumbed so easily to the concepts, thoughts, ideas and temptations that Satan and his demons had put into their minds. They played their various roles with the venom and hatred for which the powers of darkness had hoped. Now the scene was set for the final drama that would destroy the Incarnation and establish satanic rule for all time upon the Earth.

Satan called his most senior officers to an Orders Group for the purpose of planning the final act of the most significant drama that had ever been set upon the world's stage. The leading players had already been chosen and now he knew that what was required was one more concerted effort. Then he would be able to bring down the curtain that would plunge the world into the darkness of the deepest abyss and give him the absolute power and control he craved.

They met in the bowels of the earth. In a cave that Satan felt sure would guarantee that angels would not overhear them. With two massive demons standing guard at the entrance the meeting began.

Just a Field Marshal and six Generals were commanded to be present and they had knelt and worshipped their Lord Satan for a long time, before the Prince of Darkness felt sufficiently honoured by them to allow the business of the day to proceed.

The interior of the cave was in almost complete darkness, just the way Satan liked it. A ring of small lit torches around the perimeter, provided the only light and which showed nothing more than outlines. An atmosphere of intolerance and hatred prevailed.

The air in the cave was heavy with the smell of sulphur,

which always seemed to accompany demons of high rank. It was cold and growing colder as they emitted their icy contribution to the atmosphere. As was very usual when Satan himself was present, the overriding ambience was of fear. The demons did everything they could to disguise its presence with a cavalier attitude but knew that beneath the thin veneer of civilised communication, there was always the possibility of their imminent execution.

Satan allowed these very senior officers the privilege of sitting on their shields and waited while they made themselves comfortable. Then, standing in front of them so that he towered over them, he began the process of planning the final portion of the campaign that would bring the eradication of the Incarnation and give him total victory over the Earth.

"You have all done well," he began, "but do not think that I will not eliminate you if the final part of our war on righteousness is not completely successful." He paused for effect and allowed his words to take root in their minds. Then he moved across to where his silhouette appeared stark and hideous in the meagre light and outlined his strategy for the final destruction of the Man God.

His voice sounded like the growl of a bear attacking its prey and he spoke with sulphurous fumes dribbling from his mouth. He began, "I have examined Him thoroughly looking for any ground in Him that we can occupy. There is none! I have looked Him up and down and know there are no flaws in his character and nothing in Him that we can use to our advantage. His purity is an anathema to me but we will break Him," Satan paused and looked into the faces of his most senior commanders as if challenging them to disagree with him in any way. Then he added, "by the use of betrayal!"

He now moved to his left until he stood directly in front of a fully armoured demon of both massive and fearsome proportions, looking directly into the crimson slits of his eyes said, "Field Marshall Corrupticus has had those under his authority, working on a particular way forward for us. Field Marshall, explain the plan, if you would please."

The gruff and deep voiced reply of, "Yes, my Lord," came instantly and Corrupticus rose to his feet and addressed those present. "For some time now we have been looking for a way to take Him out. A great deal of time and effort has gone into preparing a strategy so that when we move against Him we can be assured of success. Nothing less than His death will suffice and we are preparing the most painful of deaths for Him. However, I'm allowing my enthusiasm to carry me away and first we must have Him firmly in our grasp."

Corrupticus stopped and glowed with hatred as he considered what he was about to say and the importance of the next part of the plan. He continued, "For some years He has been moving around the countryside with a band of followers, and we have identified one of them that we believe can be bribed. The weaknesses within him we have identified as a love of money, coupled with a strong desire to see the Incarnation become an Earthly ruler.

This man believes that if the Incarnation is put under sufficient pressure He will call His followers to arms and they will rise up under His command and drive the Romans from Palestine. My agents have been developing this man to our best possible advantage. He will be offered a sum of money that he can't possibly refuse. Then he will identify our target, pointing Him out to the Temple Guards to make sure we get the right man. He will believe he is doing the right thing, by providing the spark that will ignite the nationalistic flame that simmers beneath the surface of their society. He is mistaken in this belief, but his actions we will use to our very great advantage."

He paused and growled softly to himself and then continued, "I have arranged for them to make the arrest at night when most of His followers will not be around. To make the betrayal even more delicious, it will be done with a kiss. You might say; 'the kiss of death'." To make his point the Field Marshall kissed the palm of his enormous hand that was covered with a glove of chain mail and blew the kiss towards his subordinates. The sniggers and sneers that passed for humour among them told him that they appreciated the gesture and understood its significance.

Corrupticus paused and resumed a serious demeanour before continuing, "My demons have been working long hours amongst the religious leaders. I am confident that the High Priest and most members of their senior decision making group, a council known as the Sanhedrin, have been sufficiently influenced to condemn Him when He is tried before them.

We have already prepared several witnesses that will give false evidence against Him to ensure a conviction on a charge of blasphemy. Do you have any questions so far gentlemen?" There was a general murmuring of assent to what they were hearing.

Then General Sadisticus cleared his throat and spoke,

"There is one thing on which I am not clear, Sir," he said. "I have always understood that it is only the Roman Governor that has the authority to pronounce the death sentence on these people and he is not going to be interested in a charge of blasphemy. The Romans consider those finer points of religion to be in the hands of the local leaders. They will surely want them to deal with what the Governor will see as a relatively minor matter. After all, we have got the Romans worshipping a great many gods and all their worship of idols and false deities flows down to our Lord Satan anyway." Sadisticus stopped speaking and hoped he had not gone too far, but somehow had not been able to prevent his query sounding like criticism, but that was just him.

The Field Marshall placed his right hand on the jewel-encrusted hilt of his sword and pushed it forward but made no attempt to draw it. However, it made the point to Sadisticus that he had gone far enough and had better not go any further if he valued his life.

"You make a good point, General," Field Marshall Corrupticus said, nodding his head towards Sadisticus in an acknowledgement that maintained the veneer of collegiality between them, with both of them understanding that at a deeper level there was serious hostility.

Field Marshall Corrupticus continued, "Let me explain how we intend overcoming that legal limitation. Once He has been arrested and condemned by His own people, we will be in the background ensuring that they continue to want nothing less than His death. Then, we will inspire them to take Him to the Roman Governor who has the power to Him put to death."

Corrupticus now paused and looked down at Sadisticus whilst raising a bushy eyebrow and fixing him with the penetrating gaze, from his beady red eyes which caused even Sadisticus' black heart to miss a beat, and brought him swiftly back under the Field Marshall's authority.

Sadisticus was in no way challenging Corrupticus but he could still see a flaw in the plan and wanted very much to be on the victorious side and not be cast into the fires of Hell for all eternity. So, with a submissive demeanour he raised his hand from his knee where it had rested to indicate that he wished to ask another question. The Field Marshall saw the movement and leaning menacingly towards him growled, "What is it now, General?"

Sadisticus made sure he had the correct tone in his voice and speaking quietly said submissively, "Sir, there is still the problem of the blasphemy charge. As I see it, the Roman governor will think it insufficient for a death sentence." Corrupticus narrowed his eyes and drew in his breath through clenched teeth. He lowered his massive bony head until it was within an inch or two of Sadisticus' face. The General could smell the Field Marshall's foul breath invading the air he was breathing, then he spoke, "Do you take me for a fool?" General Sadisticus remained quite still and outwardly calm but within his armour covered chest, his heart raced and he felt the knot of fear in his stomach and he knew to remain silent. The other generals watched fascinated, hoping they were about to witness the violent death of their colleague. They hated him almost as much as they did Satan who stood behind them not saying a word but taking in everything that was happening.

The Field Marshall spat his answer into Sadisticus' face and watched his black saliva landing on its target, "I am very aware General that the Romans would never condemn a man to death on a charge of blasphemy, but it will be used initially to get the Sanhedrin involved and active. Then the charge will change to one of sedition when He goes before the Governor. The Romans are very sensitive to anything that might threaten the security of the territories they are trying to keep under submission. Particularly if we can convince them that in not putting Him to death, a wedge will be driven between the Roman Governor and his master, the Roman Emperor. On that charge General, and in those circumstances General, they will not simply put him to death, but will," a pause followed and then he shouted into Sadisticus' face, *"Crucify Him!"*

The cave erupted into a cacophony of growls of satanic delight as swords were rattled against shields, in appreciation of the mind picture each had of their great enemy receiving His due. Corrupticus followed his statement with a low growl that spoke volumes to Sadisticus, who continued to be silent and still, not daring to even wipe the flexes of black slime from his face and shoulders where they had struck him. Corrupticus knew that he had carried the day and now contentedly withdrew his head from its close proximity to Sadisticus' face. He straightened his back before adding, "Let us hope General, that it will not be General, for me to have you... nailed to a wooden cross, General!"

One of those present who had not spoken so far was General Vindicticus and he now rose to his feet. His venomous features were squat and scaly and all knew his reputation for brutal cruelty. He cleared his throat and expertly spat dark green and black bile into the darkness behind him; then turning to face forward again addressed the Field Marshall. His voice was naturally dark and menacing, "If I could raise something that is bothering me Sir, it may be a point of clarification for a number of us."

He paused to allow Field Marshal Corrupticus to nod his permission for him to continue then he noisily sucked in air through his large nostrils before doing so. He began, "In the campaign so far we have fought many angels and destroyed any number of human beings, but can we destroy the immortal. *I challenge that!"* The hairs on Corrupticus' neck rose in aggravation as he anticipated another confrontation with yet another General, he spun round to face him with a fiery determination to deal brutally with any dissention.

As he did so he reached under his shield and his left hand came out holding the handle of a mace and chain. He straightened to his full height and as he did so he drew the spiked iron ball back, causing it to reach the full extent of the chain to which it was attached; the ball hit the wall behind him with a resounding thud. The spikes did their work and embedded the ball in the shale wall.

The swiftness of his action and the severity of the result acted as a trigger and General Vindicticus, believing himself to be under attack, sprang into action in his own defense. His thorny hand reached automatically over his head for the hilt of the sword he carried in a sheath secured on his back between his shoulder blades. He grasped the sword's hilt and the black ebony blade was half drawn, when the Field Marshall pivoted lightly on the balls of his cloven feet and flung his right arm outward from across his chest.

The thin bladed dagger secured in a sheath strapped to his forearm and hidden by the sleeve of his tunic, received the impetus it needed to fling it at lightning speed and with superb accuracy, into the small gap between the plates of Vindicticus' body armour. The slender blade penetrated to its full depth leaving the hilt protruding from the General's midriff. Green slime sprang from its point of entry.

The General gasped and releasing the hilt of the half drawn sword screamed in a parody of surprise, anger, hatred and pain. His hideously crusty features contorted into a death mask as he pitched forward onto General Sadisticus, who had no time to move from the path of his falling colleague. The sound made by his armoured body colliding with Sadisticus reverberated off the walls of the cave.

The attack had occurred so suddenly that for a second or two no one moved apart from the Field Marshall, who leaned forward aggressively with a gesture that challenged the other generals to pit their fighting skills against his, if they dared. From out of the darkness at the back of the group the voice of authority spoke, "Gentlemen, gentlemen, if we continue like this it will be us that will be neutralised and not the Incarnation."

Satan moved around to the front of the group and taking hold of Vindicticus' breastplate, lifted him effortlessly and flung him against the cave's wall as if he were rubbish to be disposed of quickly. He made no further mention of the incident but carried on as if the death of one of his generals was of no consequence to him, which in reality was true. "Field

Marshall do relax and sit down, there is something I wish to say," Satan intoned evenly.

"The concern that General Vindicticus was endeavouring to clarify, does I believe, involve the status of the Incarnation and whether or not we are plotting to destroy a man or a Deity." He paused to allow the significance of his words to sink in. Then he continued, "I am very aware that when we were part of the heavenly realm, we all knew the Incarnation personally and clearly understood that He was part of the Godhead and was very much immortal." Satan paused and spat yellow and green slime into the earth between his feet and ground it in with his left heel, as he symbolically vented his feelings and demonstrated how he felt about the Godhead.

Feeling somewhat better he continued, "However, when the Incarnation became human He laid aside His glory and now functions as an ordinary man" His voice dropped to a low growl as he said, "and this is most important. In His capacity as a man we can," then he punched his right foreleg into the air and shouted in anticipation of their victory, *"put Him to death!!"* The cave erupted in a mass of growls, hoots and cheers of affirmation as they visualised the blood, agony and degradation they were soon to inflict on the best that Heaven had to offer.

The lifeless body of General Vindicticus lay crumpled against the wall of the cave with the dagger's handle protruding from it and blood oozing into a green slimy pool. None of them gave him a second thought.

C14

THE TRIAL

The arrest of the Incarnation happened just as they had planned. The kiss of betrayal started a sequence of events that moved rapidly towards trial and conviction for which a grandstand view was necessary.

Satan and Field Marshall Corrupticus sat together on the roof of Caiaphas, the High Priest's house, watching and hearing everything that was happening. Satan had positioned his most powerful generals in a circle around the house. They poured their spiritual venom of hatred down into the High Priest, the Sanhedrin and the gathered crowd. Behind the generals were row upon row of demons supporting their commanders and focusing their evil spiritual energy into the events occurring below. At the same time they provided a "black energy shield" around and over Caiaphas' house that would be very difficult for angelic warriors to penetrate.

In the sky above them, Satan's elite Early Interception Force was positioned and ready. These were demons that had proved their allegiance and skill in combat, who were ready to give their lives in the service of the Prince of Darkness. They flew a holding pattern that crisscrossed the sky as they patrolled looking out for attacking angels. They flew in sections of eight, each under a Section Commander, their black swords unsheathed and ready for action. They were the first line of defense against the angels that Satan felt sure were going to arrive at any moment, in an attempt to prevent harm befalling the Incarnation. Satan was very aware that his forces were outnumbered two to one. For every one of his demons there were two angels, hence the strategic concentration of demons into a "black energy shield" that was designed to make it extremely difficult for warrior angels to come to the Incarnation's rescue.

Never in the history of the planet Earth had such a powerful spiritual contrast occurred—the combined evil influences of Satan and his demons, the kiss of betrayal, the corrupt false witnesses; coupled with a preconceived guilty verdict from the High Priest and the Sanhedrin. In stark relief against this spiritual darkness, stood the innocence and purity of a righteous and holy Man.

General Vindicticus was assigned solely to the influence of Caiaphas, the High Priest. For a long time this senior religious leader had been subject to a strong demonic presence, but now there were no holds barred. Vindicticus used the ground that had been gained previously in Caiaphas, as a conduit to pour into him demonic power that would ensure the trial verdict that Satan required.

Vindicticus, shut down to everything, apart from the task in hand and empowered himself from the depths of Hell to make sure he accomplished his assignment. He was very aware of the vengeance that would descend upon him should he fail;

that thought kept him absolutely focused.

When the false witnesses had been heard concerning the charge of blasphemy, the Incarnation had replied truthfully and Caiaphas had declared his pre-prepared "Guilty" verdict. The first phase of the plan to put the Incarnation to death was accomplished. All the demons breathed a silent sigh of relief but knew that they could not yet relax. Each general had carefully briefed those under their command, they were to remain on full alert and provide Dark Shield Cover over the locations where the action was taking place.

A guilty verdict at a local level was one thing, but now the task was to convince the Roman authorities that the Incarnation was deserving of death. The Roman Governor held that power, now the demon commanders focused all their spiritual influence on motivating the religious leaders to take the Incarnation before that man and bring their revised accusations.

General Sadisticus had been right when he had said the Romans would not be interested in the religious charge of blasphemy. Now the task that faced the host of Hell, was to cause the High Priest and the Sanhedrin to change their accusation to one of sedition. A charge that would gain the Roman Governor's attention because of his sensitivity to civil unrest and his desire to prevent any more disruption and disorder from breaking out. A governor's reputation, in the eyes of the Roman senate, was largely dependent upon his ability to administer his province and keep it subdued, without having to ask the State for extra troops, with all the associated costs.

Part of Satan's forward planning was to appoint Major

Violenticus to come to the forefront of the action with his company of mind-bending demons. They were very skilled in the art of influencing the thought life of human beings and causing them to think in the way that served satanic purposes. They had acquired a great deal of experience over the years and now brought their abilities to bear on the religious leaders. Their technique was one of individualised attention; now Major Violenticus assigned a demon to control the thinking of the significant players as the drama unfolded in the scene below them.

These demons understood their role was to turn a group of normally rational people, who just days before had lauded and praised the Incarnation, into a hate filled mob. A mob with irrational thought which operated with a common mind, that disregarded any logic and focused its violent energies on its victim. These mind-bending demons combined into a morass of corrupt intention and evil endeavour, causing the mob to behave like a shoal of fish being harassed by sharks. They would think and move without reason in the direction that the demons drove them, as they became the catalyst of the whole operation. A mob that had a singleness of purpose and a strong determination to achieve its own desires, was able to put a civil authority under significant pressure.

The tip of the wedge was now in place and as the demons drove it home. It would have the potential to separate the Governor from his masters in Rome and no governor could afford to allow that to happen. He would see the danger to his relationship with Caesar and would know he could not allow the blow to strike, that would drive in that wedge. To prevent that from happening he would have to comply with the wishes of the mob, or civil unrest with all its consequences would break out.

The scene now changed to the Governor's residence. With great stealth the demons also moved to that location. The priests and Pharisees were the principle targets for they held a natural authority over the people, who were very used to following the lead they provided.

To make sure the mob thought and acted as required, each of the leading players was assigned a demon from the company. Major Violenticus personally briefed those under his command and was very specific in the orders he gave. Each demon was left in no doubt as to the importance of ensuring the Governor was sufficiently influenced, to decree the death penalty and clearly understood the consequences if that did not happen. Satan had made it plain that either the Incarnation was crucified or the Major and all those he commanded would be!

It was well understood that Roman governorship, was a political appointment and carried with it all the corrupting trappings of power and this one was no exception. But what Satan had not taken sufficiently into account, was the strength of the Roman legal system and its intrinsic fairness, that required evidence to support any guilty verdict that was being sought.

The Incarnation was brought before the Governor and questioned, but no reason for condemnation was found. No hard evidence existed and the Governor was of a mind to release Him. For a moment there was near panic among the demons who only just controlled the situation by intensifying their influence, regarding the implantation of sedition, into the minds of the mob. This caused them to shout their lies even more strongly concerning the riots and civil unrest, of which the Incarnation was accused and how it had started in Galilee then spread throughout the southern state of Judea.

Like a drowning man reaching for a life raft, the Governor saw a chance to extract himself from the clutches of the mob by referring the Incarnation's case to Herod, the ruler of Galilee; who happened to be in the city at the time. The Incarnation was a Galilean and was therefore under Herod's jurisdiction. He thought, "Let somebody else have this problem. I don't need it."

The Governor was only too willing to allow his soldiers to provide the escort and the Incarnation found himself in front of Herod. In the realm of the spirit, Satan's forces were in a state of high anxiety as they saw all that they had planned slipping away from them.

Herod was a brutal and immoral man whom demons had inhabited from a young age. It was they who had inspired and shaped him and led him further and further into debauchery and wickedness. They had established his character and rewarded him with control of a Region with power over the people living within its borders.

When the messenger arrived informing Herod that the Incarnation was being brought before him, he felt pleasure and delight rising from within. For some time now he had heard of this man and had been told of the miraculous works that he had performed, but the cynic in him said, "Seeing is believing." He had questioned two men after they had supposedly been healed of leprosy and they had dared to suggest that the reverse of this logic was actually true and that, "Believing was seeing". He had dealt severely with those two and left them in no doubt as to who held the valid opinion!

Now fate had placed this man under his jurisdiction and he was looking forward to meeting him. Perhaps, if the gods smiled, he could be persuaded to perform a miracle or two as a demonstration of his spiritual prowess. If that were to happen, it was just possible that the ruler of Galilee might condescend to allow himself to be convinced.

He made sure his robe was correctly positioned around him and that he looked regal, seated on a golden throne in the centre of the large reception hall. His attendant ministers and guards formed a human shield that would safeguard his person should anything untoward happen. Although he was assured that restraining chains were being used, one could never be too careful in these matters.

When the man entered he was surprised at his demeanour, so quiet, gentle and composed. For one who was accused of sedition, for which the penalty was death by crucifixion, he behaved with amazing self-control and composure. Herod launched into a series of questions designed to bring on the miracle that he wanted so much to see, but was perplexed by the Incarnation's silence and calmness.

A whole series of questions later, this Jewish rabbi, who had been so vocal wherever he went, had not uttered a word. Herod inwardly admired the peace and tranquility of the man's countenance, which stood in stark contrast to his own pride and pompous self-importance.

The man's silence continued and no progress was made. Herod began to feel that he was starting to look somewhat ineffectual and that was a feeling he did not like, for he prided himself on always being in control. He knew that the man's accusers were waiting in the wings to play their part in this drama and now he felt the moment was right to bring them on stage and thereby re-affirm his control.

Herod, was really a man with only one tool in his toolkit and that was a hammer. Now the silent man, who stood so patiently before him was going to discover what it was like to be a nail! The hammer was about to strike him hard and drive him down.

The first to bring their accusations were the Chief Priests and Caiaphas, who swept into the scene with his robes flowing and his righteous indignation filling the huge hall. Other priests followed in his wake, with the teachers of the law following behind in close attendance. They endeavoured to establish their status by speaking of being the authority of God on Earth and the mouthpiece of the Almighty, as the interpreters of the Torah, the Jewish Books of the Law.

Herod looked on as they ranted and raved about how this man had blasphemed and claimed, that should Solomon's temple be destroyed he could rebuild it in three days. Had the work of building that magnificent place of worship, not taken a large team of skilled workers forty-seven years? Herod watched this performance with a soft smirk playing around his lips. "These religious people," he thought, "are really very amusing, but is this all they have to offer by way of evidence? I thought this man was accused of insurgency and violence against the

State of Rome, but it's quite apparent to me that he couldn't fight his way out of an empty wineskin! A deluded fool he may be, but a revolutionary leader that Rome needs to fear, not in a million years."

However, Herod's eyes opened wide when accusations came forth that this man had claimed to be the King of the Jews. "Now this is more interesting," he thought, "but how can a man be a king without royal robes and subjects fawning before him. This man has none of that. He is far too gentle and introverted to fill the kingly role and where are his bodyguards and soldiers? Every king has about him military forces that will fight for him. No, this man is none of these things, but let's have some fun with him anyway. It'll make me look good in front of my guards and they'll enjoy it as compensation for having been awakened so early in the day. Then I can get on with my breakfast."

With a wave of his hand, Herod summoned the commander of the guards to his side and gave him instructions to remove the accused to another room where he would be out of earshot. Then to have a fine linen and silk robe brought from his wardrobe and put upon Him.

Whilst they waited he told everyone present that they were heartedly mistaken, if they thought he was going to take seriously the charges that they had brought against the accused and that Roman justice required solid evidence not the babblings of over inflated religious egos. The high priests and their party of underlings tried to protest, but Herod was not having any of that kind of nonsense and only had to have his guards move quickly and menacingly towards them for order to be re-established.

Then the accused was brought in wearing the kingly robe, that looked so out of place on Him and the mood quickly changed to one of derision, as they made fun of Him. The guards made rude jokes at his expense and ragged him, pushing him around and pulling his beard. Herod enjoyed himself immensely and encouraged his men in their rough banter, but through it all could not understand why the man's patience and composure remained so complete. When he began to feel hungry he stopped the rough play that was going on and after giving instructions that the man was to be returned to the Governor, went and ate a hearty breakfast.

The demons watching all this were mortified that the Incarnation had not been condemned to death and knew that their heads were on the chopping block. When Major Violenticus reported the outcome of the Incarnation's trial before Herod to Satan, it was as if a volcano was simmering, getting ready to erupt.

At first the Great Demon received the report with almost total disbelief and then he started to pace up and down and fume. As the magnitude of the situation settled upon him, so his mood darkened and he began cursing and blaspheming.

Finally, the eruption came and he screamed profanities at the top of his voice. He all but lost control completely as he kicked, punched and spat at every object within striking distance. His personal bodyguards quaked in fear and did their best to stay out of sight. When the pressure had been relieved and Satan's temper had subsided somewhat, the small servant demons of the household, moved around as quietly and as inconspicuously as they could; while they cleaned and tidied the mess until things appeared normal again.

When his composure had fully returned Satan realised that time was passing and that events surrounding the Incarnation were moving ahead. Having been taken again before the Governor, a decision was about to be made concerning the Incarnation's fate and it was not looking good.

The leading player in the drama was undoubtedly the Governor himself. For it was he who had the power to condemn the Incarnation to death, but it was obvious that he had seen through the lies and self-seeking fabrications that had been presented as evidence, and was totally unconvinced to the level of guilt. Action needed to be taken quickly if the powers of darkness were to control his decision and have him bring down the verdict they wanted.

The Governor was a strong-minded man, who was following a course that was in line with the well-established Roman legal system and was unlikely to deviate from the pursuit of justice. "No," Satan reasoned, "my best chance of success does not lie with the Governor but with the mob. I must succeed or the righteous influences the Incarnation has initiated will spread. We risk entering an age of redemption and losing the wonderful degradation of humanity I have worked so hard to achieve." Looking around he saw Major Violenticus skulking in the background and summoned him into his presence.

Their conversation was brief and to the point as the Major received precise instructions, that were to achieve the desired result or bring about the Major's demise in the most painful and protracted way possible. Major Violenticus cringed inwardly at the thought of being fed feet first through a meat slicer and moved quickly to ensure his Company of mind-control demons fulfilled their function with the mob. If they didn't he would make sure their end was in line with his own.

Events were now moving rapidly towards a conclusion and an acquittal. The Governor was on his feet addressing the crowd and saying that neither he nor Herod had found any reason to condemn the man. It was at this point, that a dark spiritual influence slid silently into position above them. In an endeavour to appease the crowd's bloodlust but save the Man's life, the Governor said he would have the man whipped before releasing him. Now the spiritual atmosphere changed dramatically as mind-controlling influences of the most powerful kind were directed at the assembled crowd. The specialist demons above them acted together and a concentration of satanic spiritual energy, of immense proportions was released and directed at the people standing in front of the Governor.

The crowd was instantly transformed into a mob of shouting, screaming maniacs, as the massive pulse of evil energy, created hatred and vengeance deep in their minds. As it came upon them it overpowered their ability to think logically and penetrated to the very core of their thought life.

They were now united in a common cause like never before. Priests, teachers of the law and ordinary people were welded into a focused entity that had one purpose and one purpose only, to bring about the death of the Incarnation. The Governor was shocked and overwhelmed by the volume, intensity and magnitude of their shouts and screams of, *"Crucify him!*

Crucify him! Crucify him!

Absolutely perplexed by the scene before him and what he was hearing, the Governor tried once more to prevent what he knew would be a travesty of justice. Shouting to be heard above the roar of the crowd, he asked again, **"But what crime has he committed? I can find no wrong in this man deserving of death! I shall order Him whipped and released."**

The demons above the crowd now pulled out all the stops, as Major Violenticus pointed with a black encrusted, claw-like finger at the platoon he was holding in reserve and ordered them into the fray. The increase in demonic power was instant, as it flowed downward into the people and motivated them totally to scream at the top of their lungs for the Incarnation to be crucified.

Feeling that he was being controlled by a mob and hating to be manipulated in that way, the Governor clung to the concept of justice that the practice of Roman law had placed so strongly within him. He tried another way to prevent the death of an innocent man. Taking a deep breath and raising his voice above the noise of the crowd, he said loudly, **"At this time of the year it is customary for me to release to you a prisoner for whom you ask. I will release to you this man."**

The crowd again became a mob as the chief priests, inspired by their demon masters, stirred them to ask for the release not of the Incarnation, but of a man named Barabbas, who had been found guilty of murder. They shouted his name over and over again, "Barabbas! Barabbas! Barabbas! Barabbas! Release to us Barabbas!"

The Governor could resist their will no longer, as he too

started to succumb to the pervading spiritual atmosphere. It acted like a black covering that knew only the will and desires of total demonic intent. He felt confused and overwhelmed and like a man in a trance, gave in to the evil pressure that was upon him and instructed that Barabbas be released.

In one desperate and final attempt he addressed the crowd once more and pointing to the Incarnation asked, **"And what shall I do with this Man?"** The mob's response was again instantaneous as they shouted and screamed, *"Crucify him! Crucify him! Crucify him! Crucify him!"* Feeling there was nothing more that he could do to save the man's life, and fearing the political consequences of riot and mayhem, he passed the sentence that Satan wanted—and for which the mob bayed. He ordered the Incarnation to be crucified.

Now, the Governor wanted only to be free of the sickening feeling in his stomach. Turning on his heel left the scene, knowing that he had sentenced an innocent man to death and betrayed the trust placed in him to administer justice.

Hearing the sentence and seeing him go, Major Violenticus breathed a deep sigh of relief and gave the signal that allowed his demons to cease their intense activity. His order came just in time, as they were all nearing exhaustion and could not have sustained their maximum effort very much longer. The platoon commanders gave their orders and the mind bending Company relaxed, left to regroup and rest in preparation for their next assignment.

Solders came and led the Incarnation away to his fate and Satan and the hosts of Hell rejoiced hideously!

C15

CRUCIFIXION

Events now moved rapidly. The focus changed and the contrast could not have been starker. From a scene of imperial splendour with the Governor, his magnificent home and his entourage of obedient attendants, to the adjacent stables and the whipping post at their rear.

The personnel also differed markedly, gone were the clean flowing robes of government officialdom and the manners of civilised high society. They were replaced by the smell of horses, manure and the roughly dressed soldiers of an army of occupation, with their even rougher behaviour. These men were far from home and cared little for the people in whose land they now found themselves. They served their military masters wherever they were assigned and in whatever way they were commanded.

Strong arms and hands calloused from rough work, now grabbed the Incarnation and removed His outer garment. Ribald remarks followed one another and course jokes were made at His expense. A leather thong bound His wrists and was tied through the hole in the top of the stout, blood streaked post set in the cobble-stoned courtyard. Around the base of which were the blood and excrement stains from previous floggings.

The Centurion stood off to one side to oversee the process, as two well-built soldiers readied themselves in preparation for the exertions required of them. They were men hardened by the brutality of warfare. Their battles were fought at close quarters with the enemy and hand-to-hand combat was normal in their soldiering. They neither asked for mercy nor gave any. They had seen many bloodthirsty sights and the savage injuries inflicted on the battlefield, where limbs were pierced and severed, blood flowed freely and the groans and screams of the injured and dying were commonplace.

In a macabre way they revelled in the task before them, for it singled them out as senior members of a battle hardened community of fighting men. It gave them a particular status above their peers, as it confirmed their superior's view of them as physically strong men who could be trusted with a particularly brutal role.

Each spent a moment or two checking the flagellum they would use. They ensured the binding on the handle of the whip was secure and the thirteen, long thin leather strands were securely in place. These thongs held the pieces of lead and bone along their length that would open up the skin of the unfortunate's back and body. This they knew would happen, as they laid them across him with all the style and strength they possessed.

They were aware there was a strong possibility that the man would die at their hands. For often the injuries and shock inflicted by the flagellum would stop a man's heart and occasionally death would occur through loss of blood. It mattered not to them, for the man was going to die anyway but they would try not to kill him too soon. Crucifixion had a certain process about it that they enjoyed and anyway it relieved the boredom of barrack life routine.

The Centurion's deep strong voice now rang out across the courtyard, causing them to quickly complete their preparations and take their positions either side of the man. *"Punishment detail. Ready,"* he shouted. They each gripped their flagellum and at the command, *"Commence punishment!"* their work began.

At the first stroke the man screamed at the initial shock of the lash striking him. From then on the body before them became more and more a bloodied mess as the whips in their hands did their work.

After a few minutes the man could no longer stand and hung from the top of the post with the leather thong supporting his weight. He cried and whimpered with each successive stroke of the whip. The exertion caused them to perspire and they removed their outer tunics and continued their rhythmic brutality, as they harmonised together in the flaying of a human body, that now resembled nothing more than a piece of butchered meat!

Again the centurion's voice was heard, "Cease punishment." This was the signal for another soldier to step forward. He carried a leather bucket full of water, which he threw over the bloody torso.

The centurion now stepped forward and grasping the man's hair, pulled his head back to see if he was alive or dead. Seeing the glimmer of life still in the man's eyes he stepped back and ordered him untied.

Now the wooden cross that stood against the buildings' stonewall, became the focus and the man was led to it. He was a pitiful sight with a mass of open and bleeding wounds all over His upper body. Chunks of skin and muscle had been torn out and bloody lines, left by the lash had reduced His back to not much more than pulp. The Centurion again gripped the man's hair and pointing his face at the rough wood, ordered, *"Carry it!"*

The soldiers held the cross up and with the little remaining strength he had, the man put his shoulder under it. Somehow he got control and with a soldier either side, giving balance and direction, began to walk forward with staggering steps on his final journey.

The soldiers on sentry duty now opened the large wooden gates in the courtyard wall. The expectant crowd waiting outside, cheered and roared as he came into their view. As the small procession passed through the gates the people thronged about him laughing, cursing and shouting caustic and ribald remarks, enjoying in a brutal way the suffering of another human being.

In the realm of the spirit, Satan's Early Interception Force moved backward and forward, crisscrossing the sky above and expecting at any moment an attack that signalled an angelic rescue attempt. Below them, the demons that comprised Dark Shield Cover remained in position. They provided the venom and hatred that spurred the crowd to turn a man's agonising death, into something almost carnival-like, but without the joyous atmosphere. In its place was an overlay of sinister celebration that the demons kept energised, as events moved relentlessly towards the Incarnation's death and the fulfilment of Satan's desires.

In the heavenly realm the archangel Michael was exercising great restraint. His natural motivation was strongly towards the protection and defense of the Incarnation of the God that he loved and served, but the Father's instructions to him were clear. He had been told that this was the Father's will and that under no circumstances was he to interfere. He watched the proceedings below with the archangel Gabriel, standing beside him. They were both experiencing a deep-seated anger that was coupled with their falling tears. As they saw the Incarnation being brutalised, they felt something of the agony He was experiencing.

Their tears flowed freely. They itched to use their flaming swords on the demons they knew they could vanquish with the forces at their disposal. However, the Father's word was their command and they would be obedient to it as they held their anger in check.

The great warrior Michael was the first to speak and as he did so, the tips of his wings trembled and shook, manifesting the emotion he felt even though he was doing his best to exercise self-control. With quavering voice he said, "How can we watch this happening and do nothing to prevent it? I'd just love to use my warriors and get stuck into those demons. They'd soon feel the cutting edge of our swords and we'd very quickly vanquish them and stop this obscenity."

Gabriel put his arm across his friend's shoulders to comfort him and express his solidarity with him. He tried to put the situation into the Father's perspective. "Isn't love a strange thing," he said, "who would have thought the Father would have gone to these lengths, to provide those rebellious humans with a way back into relationship with Him? It surely says to me that love is not a feeling but an act of the will. I think I would have been inclined to wipe them out once and for all and be done with them. But the Father has a different way of doing things and wants to offer them the depth of His love and His redeeming grace. Don't really understand it myself, but ours is not to reason why..." and he left the sentence unfinished.

Michael drew in a deep breath and did his best to control his emotions before replying, "But to go through all this pain and suffering, is it really necessary? You'd think there'd be another way, wouldn't you?" Gabriel didn't respond immediately but paused, wondering how best to express the truth he understood so clearly, and then broke the silence between them by saying, "Michael, it's all about redeeming love and paying the price for what they have done. He's taking upon Himself the punishment they deserve."

His words provoked a quick fire response, "But what an enormous price He's paying and it's not over yet, the worst is still to come!" Michael responded, gripping the hilt of his sword longing to draw it. Gabriel counselled, "Steady on my friend. Don't let your emotions get in the way of what is actually the Father's defined process. Their redemption is all about sacrifice. You know as well as I do that the price of sin must be paid for in the shedding of blood. Either they pay for it by being eternally separated from Him. Or, He pays for it like this and provides a way for them to return to fellowship with Him. It's all about love, Michael, and the Father loves them so much."

The small procession moved slowly along the track that led to the Place of the Skull, outside the city wall, where crucifixions and stoning were traditionally carried out. The crowd pressed in and their venomous hatred was shouted and spat at the blood-soaked Man, struggling under the weight of a wooden cross. Soon He would be nailed to that cross, and they would be bonded in death.

The soldiers were constantly pushing the marauding mob out of their path to clear the way forward. Their tempers were becoming more and more frayed by the crowd's constant pressure upon them.

The brutality that had been inflicted upon the Incarnation by the flagellum, had caused terrible injuries and His body had suffered incredible stress from the whipping He had endured. His strength was waning and finally gave out as He stumbled and fell under the weight of the wooden cross. He lay in the dirt only semiconscious. Soldiers lifted the cross from Him knowing that He was incapable of going any further under its weight.

The centurion now exercised his authority as a Roman officer and looking around saw standing close by, a well-built young man who was on his way into the city. The man was unaware of the background to what was happening and looked perplexed and confused, but his feelings were not important to a soldier. The centurion pointed to him and said, "You! Yes you, get your shoulder under that cross and carry it, or you'll feel my sword!"

Around this procession of death, the demons providing Black Shield Cover, continued to produce a spiritual screen that maintained a demonic atmosphere of tangible evil that precluded goodness, in any form, manifesting its presence. Hatred and bitterness held sway under the prevailing influences. Those who had been closest to the Incarnation throughout His years of ministry, lost their courage and melted into the background.

Satan, with Field Marshall Corrupticus, and eleven of his closest Generals, formed a spiritual concentration that produced an intense inner sphere of demonic power and darkness. This was the epicenter of satanic activity that surrounded the leading players, in the most important event ever to occur. They focused their attention on those closest to the Incarnation and precluded any inherent righteousness from coming to the fore. They knew their moment of triumph was at hand and were determined that nothing should detract from their complete and final victory.

The execution squad now arrived at Golgotha, the Place of the Skull, and there in the city rubbish dump the Lord of the Universe was crucified. He was nailed to a wooden cross that was raised high between the crosses of two criminals, who were to die with him. The spiritual conditions were now so strongly established that it was easy for Satan to torment Him, even as He hung there, in the most incredible agony and with His life slipping away.

The Roman Governor had written His title, "King of the Jews" in three languages and the parchment had been nailed to the wood above His head. Those of the mob that gathered at the foot of His cross, read this insignia and shouted their derisive remarks at Him. The criminal, crucified on his left, took up the obscene banter and joined in the game of torment, "If you're a king, then get us down from here!"

Against this atmosphere of intense and oppressive evil that had established a countenance of darkness over the crucifixion scene, the righteousness of the Incarnation shone like a beacon on a stormy night.

The two criminals hanging from the nails driven through their wrists and feet, knew that the self-seeking and unlawful path they had chosen in life, had finally brought them what they deserved. The dying criminal on the Incarnation's right saw the reality of the situation and through all the pain and regret he was experiencing, spoke to the other, about the venomous words coming from his mouth. "What are you trying to do my friend, curse us both into Hell? We're only getting what we deserve but surely you have enough savvy to realise that he's innocent of any crime!"

Then through a haze of pain he spoke again directing his words to the Incarnation, "Lord, remember me when you come into your throne" His request was responded to immediately, with words that cut through everything that was happening and reached out into eternity. "This day you will be with me in paradise."

Satan overheard what was said and ground his teeth and growled in anger. It was now noon and the sun was climbing to its zenith, when the Father used His sovereign power and commanded it not to shine and darkness covered the land. It was as if what was happening was too cataclysmic not to be recorded in a truly significant way, yet at the same time too awful to have the eyes of men look upon it. The One through whom all creation had come, hung on a cross, dying in the most incredible agony whilst being crucified between two criminals.

The demons saw the light depart and felt secure and comfortable in the ensuing darkness. They misinterpreted completely what was happening and believed that their hour had really come. That the blackness added strength to their cause, providing them with a confirming sign of their victory over righteousness. They revelled in their success and Satan beamed and received the congratulations of his senior officers, with a smug look of contempt on his face, as he gazed in ecstasy at the scene before him.

In his black heart, Satan saw the future of the world as he envisioned the depths of degradation he could engender and the bottomless abyss, into which he would drag creation and the human race.

To make his triumph complete, all he needed was to sever the slender thread connecting the Incarnation to life. He willed it to happen and in a semi trance-like state, of almost overwhelming self-delusion, he imagined the whole of Heaven and Earth bowing the knee and worshipping him. The only thing separating him from his final goal was that spark of life within the Incarnation. Satan willed Him to die. He wanted Him dead!

Without realising he was even doing it, he focused on the cross in the centre and with his yellow eyes almost closed he said aloud, "Die, die, die, die..." The demons within earshot heard their Lord Satan's words and took up the cry. Soon every demon both great and small was mimicking their master. Their initial hushed tones grew louder and louder until that word was being shouted by every foul fiend in the universe, *"Die, die, die!!!"* The pervading spiritual atmosphere was one of incredible evil.

Here was the great God of the universe, submitted to the hands and actions of men, hanging on a cross and close to death. In this series of events the love of the Father, for His creation, was being expressed.

The physical agony being experienced by the Incarnation was extreme and yet constituted only part of His total pain. His cry of separation from the Father was soon to be shouted across time and space, for He was experiencing a far greater agony of spirit; but it had to be. For if it did not occur the sins of the world could not be dealt with. Now, in His final moments of human life, all the sin of those alive and those yet to be born, was heaped upon Him. Its effects crucified and nullified and put to death along with Him.

The Incarnation was paying the price of the sin of all those human beings alive now and in the generations to come. From here on, all that was required for humans to live eternally in the Father's nearer presence, was that they come to the Incarnation, surrender themselves to Him and seek for themselves, His kingdom and its righteousness.

Now the Incarnation raised His voice and expressed what He was experiencing. He shouted into the physical and spiritual darkness, that surrounded and enveloped Him, *"My God, my God, why have you abandoned me?"*

Then a final statement, "Into your hands I commend my spirit." And He hung His head and died.

In those few moments He opened the way for all human

beings to be reunited with the Father. The separating barrier of sin had been dealt with because His agonising sacrifice and His blood had paid the price for it.

The spiritual impact of the greatest event Heaven and Earth had ever witnessed was felt by both demons and angels. The demons, led by Satan their Commander in Chief, began to wildly celebrate the victory of evil over good. The angels all experienced incredible despair as they helplessly watched the holiest and purest human life, that had ever lived, be extinguished by evil.

The Father was unsmiling but calm. He called to His side two of His highest ranking angels for a special task. The angels He chose were magnificent beings of enormous stature and holiness. They came before Him to receive their instructions with their beautiful silken wings furled, as a mark of respect and their heads bowed, as they knelt on bended knees to be personally briefed by Him. Their pure white garments shone with an iridescent glow and the golden bands around their waists supported the weight of the jewel-encrusted scabbards, that held their golden bladed swords.

The Father spoke softly to them with the power of command that motivated and inspired. He was to launch them into their task with an impetus that no demon was ever going to deter or deflect. As the Father finished speaking they raised from their knees and having bowed, stepped backward two paces, before departing at supersonic speed to carry out their special assignment.

The two angels flew in close formation keeping a vigilant watch for demons. When they arrived at their destination, the centre of the city, they encountered a large group of demons under Colonel Profanius, desecrating the temple. Having been celebrating they were becoming quite drunk and their discipline was breaking down.

The demons were no match for the two mighty angels, who drawing their golden, scarlet tipped swords, immediately attacked line abreast. The first six or eight demons they struck were quickly dispatched by the ferocity of the encounter; seeing their compatriots falling like flies the rest fled in disarray. The two angels pursued them to the city boundary and when confident they would not return continued with what they had come to do.

Moving quickly they entered the temple and made their way through the outer courts, until they came to the inner and most sacred part, the Holy of Holies. Here they paused for a moment as a mark of respect and then entered that most sacred place. It was the room to which the High Priest came just once a year. He was the only human being permitted to do so, and then only on the Day of Atonement, to make atonement for the sins of the people. This inner sanctum was a square room that comprised stonewalls, covered with wood on three sides and with a heavy ornate brocade curtain, forming the forth side and covering the entrance way.

The angels were clear concerning the task they had been commissioned to fulfil. Now using their silken wings they raised from the ground, until they were at the top of the curtain. Then, grasping its centre they pulled against each other in opposite directions. The curtain was beautifully made of the finest materials and it was with significant effort that they completed their assignment, as they rent the curtain in two, from top to bottom and symbolically opened the way for all to enter into the most holy place, the Father's presence. They knew that what they had done was symbolising what the Incarnation's sacrificial death had achieved, in dealing with the effects of sin that separated humans from the Father.

Now the barrier of sin no longer existed. The way was unrestricted for every human being to come into the Father's presence. For in His act of supreme sacrifice, the Incarnation had taken all the sin of the world upon Himself and paid the price for it, by dying in the way that He had. The Father's redeeming love had become a tangible reality!

The curtain across the front of the Holy of Holies now hung in two pieces and the two angels stood in front of it feeling the satisfaction of a task well done. They rose together in close formation, with swords drawn in readiness to defend themselves should that become necessary, they speedily returned to the Father's presence to report the completion of their task.

This great purpose was however hidden to Satan, who saw the Incarnation's death as the means by which his own power of death had become absolute. Had he not brought about the death of the Incarnation, would not sin and death now rule supreme over mankind and throughout the world? He would exercise that life denying power over all of creation for all of eternity. He and his cohorts continued their diabolical celebration.

C16

RESURRECTION

It was dark and still in the tomb where the Incarnation had been laid after His body had been removed from the cross. The large round stone that sealed the chamber had been rolled into place. Roman soldiers stood guard outside to prevent any possibility of the Incarnation's followers removing the body and claiming He had been resurrected.

Through the Friday night and all day Saturday, the body lay on the cold stone slab. In the deep dark recesses of his kingdom, Satan and all the fallen angels were celebrating in a wild and provocative manner. The generals had brought together all their forces and the Prince of Darkness was receiving their adulation, praise and worship. They drank deeply of their success and were intoxicated by its nectar. The smell of sulphur was heavy in the air and Satan stood in the centre of a pentagram, whilst his minions cavorted and blasphemed, they entered into the deepest acts of debauchery imaginable, as they worshipped him.

They had killed the Incarnation and the power of death was now going to rise to new and previously undreamed of heights, as the completeness of degradation, baseness and filth was released. The whole of creation was poised to descend into the depths of a terrible spiritual, moral and eternal abyss, from which there was to be no returning.

Satan believed he had established within the human race, the power of death in its finality and totality and for all eternity. He had killed the Incarnation, destroyed the Father's rescue mission and eliminated any possibility of human beings living eternally with the Father, in the fullness of His kingdom. Now their physical death would also mean spiritual death and every one of them would spend eternity in Hell with him.

He glowed with demonic elation at the prospect, gloried in the images that formed in his mind of humanity locked in his evil embrace forever, with no possibility of redemption or escape. He rejoiced at the prospects the future held. The way was now open for him to have absolute power and control over the human race, to receive all the praise and adulation that he craved. The deeper implications he also clearly understood. He revelled in the prospect of every human's spirit, being subject to his fallen and depraved spirit and of his power being absolute over them.

He was in no doubt that his forces had been victorious in the battle against the Incarnation and that he had won a great victory by having Him put to death. Now, nothing stood in his way for the domination of the minds of mankind. He looked forward to releasing a reign of terror of unprecedented proportions into the world, but for now it was time to celebrate.

From the stillness and silence of His Kingdom, the Father looked upon the body of His Son and grieved that such pain and damage had been necessary. Yet, He was pleased that the Incarnation had obeyed His will and remained dedicated and true to the commission He had given Him.

It would have been so simple for the cross, with all it's suffering, to be avoided. In his humanity, the Incarnation could easily have taken another path and walked out of the city that fateful night and avoided the agony of the whip and the pain and degradation of the cross. However, He had come for a purpose and that purpose had now been fulfilled. The price for mankind's redemption from sin had been paid in full and in the only way possible, by the shedding of His most holy blood. It was now time for the Father to act and complete His redemptive plan.

The Father's power now moved sovereignly into the cavernous tomb where the body of the Incarnation lay. He prepared for the most significant act of re-creation the world was ever to experience. The Father's love for humanity was about to become manifest and the result of the Incarnation's obedience to the Father, was soon to reach out into the human race, in the most dynamic and important way possible.

As the Father's love enveloped the lifeless body of the Incarnation, the most incredible power in the universe was released. It flowed into the corpse and in microseconds the Father's re-creative energy changed death into life.

The tomb was filled with love, light and power.

As death was driven out so life entered in and resurrection occurred. In the twinkling of an eye Satan's power over death was utterly destroyed!

The Father smiled inwardly, knowing that through the

Incarnation's obedience the way for human beings to return to fellowship with Him was open. The Incarnation had paid the price for both sin and rebellion through His suffering and the shedding of His blood. He had become the acceptable sacrifice for the redemption of every human being. The obstacle of sin was now potentially removed. All that was required for humans to again live eternally in harmony with Him, was for them to choose to enter into relationship with Him and to give up their independence from Him. In doing so, they would receive His blessings and spend eternity with Him in the fullness of His kingdom. This had been made possible through the death and resurrection of the Incarnation.

Resurrection power was the most significant force the universe had ever experienced, for it flowed from the Father's heart of love for His creation and embraced all that He had created. It now pulsated and streamed instantaneously across creation and impacted the demonic, like a spiritual hammer blow. Satan and the host of Hell, felt its effect instantly and froze in mid celebration as its reality struck them. The blood drained from Satan's face as he realised what had happened. From the Field Marshalls down to the lowliest demons, all knew that their malicious hatred and vicious degradation had been defeated. Utterly destroyed and vanquished by resurrection power, flowing from the Father's heart of forgiveness and a totally sacrificial love.

The full spiritual impact of what had occurred through the Incarnation's crucifixion and resurrection became clear to Satan. The rage and anger that exploded from him, knew no bounds or restraint, as he sought to place the blame for his kingdom's defeat upon anyone but himself.

The executions he carried out of those loyal to him, were to establish a new level of fear in those he spared. His ravings reached lunatic level as his hysterics deepened and he gyrated and cannoned about, killing and destroying as he gave expression to the rage of his defeat.

His murderous fury continued unabated for a long time and when he finally calmed down he ground his teeth in anger. He consoled himself with the thought that humans still had the gift of free will. Was not he the supreme tempter? He could see no reason why he should not continue his nefarious work amongst them. He was sure that he would be able to surreptitiously influence most humans not to become part of the Father's kingdom. He was confident that he would be able to seduce the vast proportion of them with the trappings of spiritual deception, or by the power and pleasures of the material world. Thus, continuing to keep them under his influence and carrying them with him into the depths of Hell and eternal damnation.

C17
FINALITY

The disciples and followers of the Incarnation were full of expectation having seen the Incarnation alive and well on so many occasions after His resurrection from death. They had listened to Him attentively throughout the forty days He spent with them as He had taught them concerning the Kingdom of Heaven.

The Incarnation stressed that they were not to leave the city but to wait for the spiritual empowering of the Holy Spirit that the Father had promised to all who bow the knee to His Son.

The Father called to Himself two very senior angels. The robes they wore were glistening white and the halos of crystal light about their heads denoted their purity, their gold and crimson swords signified their very senior rank.

They knelt before the Father as He spoke to them, "My Son has very successfully completed the mission I set before Him and the time has come for Him to return to the fullness of my kingdom. It is most important that His disciples understand that He must leave them now but He will return in a second coming and reappear on the Earth. On that occasion he will not be coming as He did previously as the Suffering Servant but as the King of Kings and the Lord of Lords. When this occurs those loyal to Him, be they alive or sleeping in death, He will gather to Himself and bring them into my nearer presence for all eternity.

At that time Satan will be cast into an eternal lake of fire and his followers, both demon and human, will be destroyed. I want you, Michael and Gabriel, to go to His followers who are with Him at this moment and speak to them. Tell them that He will return in the same manner in which He is going to depart. He will ascend in a cloud and at His return He will descend from Heaven to Earth also in a cloud.

His second coming will be a cataclysmic event that will occur without warning. Every eye will see and every heart perceive, for as the lightning flashes from the East to the West, so shall My Son's second coming be. He will appear in His glory and My glory, also with the glory of the holy angels.

At that time My trumpet will blast forth and this will be the signal for those who have died believing in My Son to rise first. Then those who are living will be caught up together with them in the clouds to meet My Son in the air and their union with Him will be established for ever and ever."

Michael and Gabriel rose from their knees and having stepped back two paces about turned and opening their gossamer wings, flew to complete their mission leaving behind them a trail of gold and diamond pointed crystal light.

The Incarnation finished speaking to his band of followers concerning the empowering from on high that was to come upon them to equip them to witness for Him. As He did so, He lifted bodily from the ground and rose above them, rising ever upward as He ascended, returning to the glory of his Father's kingdom. Every eye was fixed upon Him and hearts fluttered with surprise and anticipation as a cloud gathered about Him and hid Him from their sight.

As this happened, Michael and Gabriel touched down among the Incarnation's followers and delivered to them the Father's message. With the Incarnation having departed from them and remembering what the angels had told them, they made their way into the city to prayerfully wait for the promised empowering of the Holy Spirit to come upon them.

In the meantime, Satan's evil mind was working overtime. He pondered what his first priority was to be in the establishment of his evil work throughout mankind. He saw quite clearly a number of possibilities, but how best to use the demonic resources he had at his disposal?

He sat on the lip of an active volcano where the smell of sulphur was strongest, an environment he always found helped him to think clearly. He asked himself where his greatest measure of success had occurred and thinking back over recent events the answer came to him almost forcibly. Had not his demons been able to influence and corrupt the minds of the people gathered before the Roman Governor and cause them to scream, *"Crucify him! Crucify him!"* Satan realised the way forward to maximising the degradation of the human race lay in his demons corrupting their thinking. Then the evil genius' mind kicked in as he thought, "Why not cause this to happen by my demons residing in human beings and influencing their thinking from within them?"

He closed his eyes and stroked his goatee beard. He revelled in the elation that he felt at the prospect of the potency of success and ground his teeth whilst rumbling deep in his throat, "Yes, yes, that's the way to do it, corrupt their thinking." The way to put his new idea into practice began formulating in his mind and never one to delay forward movement he moved quickly to put his new Strategic Plan into action.

Satan stood on cloven hoofs and looked upwards to where his Bodyguard Company was positioned. They were flying a holding pattern in the sky above him, with their swords drawn and never being far from him they provided a screen of protection. They were his fiercest demon warriors, sworn to protect him and if necessary die for him, should they encounter the warrior angels of Michael's armies.

He raised a cloven hoof in signal to his senior messenger demon, who immediately appeared before him and dropped to his knees in abeyance and submission. The instructions Satan then gave to this messenger would ensure that an Orders Group comprising his field marshals and generals would assemble before him within the hour to be told of his plan and receive their orders.

Immediately they came from every part of Satan's kingdom, trailing black smoke through the sky behind them and with fear growing in their hearts not knowing the reason for their summons. They stood in a large apprehensive group, not daring to sit or to relax in any way until given permission to do so. They emitted fear with the atmosphere around them growing ever colder and more tainted by the uncertainty in their black hearts. Their Lord and Master, Satan, left them in this condition for a full hour knowing that his stock in trade was fear, which he was so skilled at using to his best advantage.

Moving from behind the cover where he had secreted himself, Satan appeared suddenly before them. As he did so each of these high-ranking demons gasped in surprise and recovering as quickly as possible, removed their helmets and dropped to their knees before their Master. As they did so their steel and leather armour creaked and scabbarded swords clanked against the rocky ground. They emitted a cacophony of discordant sound as each one entered into the worship that Satan demanded whenever they were commanded to assemble before him.

Knowing that he was most dangerous when being congenial, the atmosphere of fear heightened, as Satan spoke in softened tones saying, "Gentlemen you may relax. I have brought you together to brief you concerning my latest initiative which is designed to bring down those ridiculous creatures we know as human beings." He spat a glob of green and black slime onto the ground in front of him to give emphasis to what he was saying and continued, "We are spirit beings and although we have the capacity to materialise, the next part of my strategic plan requires that we operate, in the spirit. Each one of you and the subordinates that you command are going to bring to bear the principal aspects of your fallen natures to where the most harm can be done. You are going to enter and live within human beings." Satan paused for effect and as he did so came murmurings of ascent and compliance from those listening. "Brilliant plan." "Amazing concept." "My Lord, when do we start?"

Satan then unfolded to his commanders the way his plan would work. Each of them were to be responsible for the satanic development of the fallen natures of the demons under their command. Whatever depth of depravity those demons were currently exhibiting it was to be heightened and their training in the art of temptation developed further. Satan explained that it was through temptation that his forces were to enter into the lives of men and women, speaking into their minds and thereby corrupting their behaviour. This master strategist of corruption and deceit enthusiastically explained that the role of every demon was now to be primarily, "temptation." Each one of them was to use the main aspect of their fallen character to corrupt the thinking of men and women and bring their thought life in line with the fallenness each demon possessed.

As he explained this Satan was aware of some puzzled looks on the hideous faces of his senior commanders. He would normally castigate them for not fully understanding what he was saying, but decided because of the importance of this new strategy, to further explain how his plan was to work.

He began again, "Let us say, that the human we are wanting to influence and corrupt has the opportunity to steal from their employer. In such a case the demons assigned to that person would do all they can to show how easy it would be to carry out the theft. Then coupled with that, the affirmation that the person was so smart, the possibility of getting caught was just about non-existent.

Now once the theft has occurred you will influence them to carry on stealing, their thefts continuing and growing greater until the entry point this behaviour has created in the person's character is large enough for the demons concerned to enter in and live within the person. From then on, temptation must be brought into other areas of the person's character; sexual fallenness and participation in the occult are always good directions to go in. The resident demons can then invite other demons to join them until maximum satanic effect has been achieved within the person's character. We are aiming for the complete corruption of every human being. Do you understand!?" There came to Satan's ears a chorus of voices giving ascent to what he had said and the rattling of their swords emphasised that they had enthusiastically understood what they had been told.

Satan stood tall and dominant over his senior officers as he closed the Orders Group with a few final words, "Every one of you will return immediately to the formations you command and explain to those demons under you our new Strategic Plan. You will also remind them of our wonderful catchphrase that we, 'Come only to steal, kill and destroy.'

His words produced an instantaneous response as the senior demons rose to their feet in one accord and repeating their master's words, screamed them at the top of their voices, *"Steal, kill and destroy. Steal, kill and destroy. Steal, kill and destroy."*

Looking upon the scene that he had created, Satan's black heart glowed with satisfaction. He felt sure he had carried his senior commanders with him. He looked forward to seeing the effects his strategic plan would have on human beings as they were brought into corruption and degradation.

In the Kingdom realms of Heaven, a totally different scenario was being enacted. The Holy Spirit was very aware of everything Satan was establishing and knew that it was time for His power and love to come into play. He had already drawn the Incarnation's followers together in one place, an upper room, where they were able to fellowship and pray with a reasonable degree of safety from the religious authorities and the civil powers.

The Incarnation's final instructions to them had been followed precisely. They prayed and waited to receive the power from on high of which He had spoken and which He had promised would come upon them.

They were one hundred and twenty in number, a mixture of working-class people, none of whom had any special status or standing in society. Yet, the Holy Spirit knew what He was about to do and the changes that His empowering would bring upon them.

He entered the room where they were gathered, coming initially as a mighty rushing wind and filling the whole house with the sound of His holy presence. Then, He came upon each one of them individually, alighting upon their heads as a tongue of fire. The empowering He imparted was life transforming.

The effect of the Holy Spirit's actions was immediate. Gone from them was fear and apprehension as the binding chains of anxiety fell from them and submission to false religious systems eliminated. In their place came a boldness borne of

Kingdom power and authority which flowed within them. Their spirits were strengthened, renewed and revitalised as they were endued with spiritual power from on high.

Each one of them responded to the Holy Spirit's influence as Holy Spirit placed within them an authority they had never known before. They felt the strength of His power of command welling up from within them and providing the impetus they needed to be ambassadors for, and a witness to, the Incarnation's life and ministry.

Simultaneously they rose to their feet. With Holy Spirit fire burning within them they knew they could be silent no longer but must bear witness to the life transforming salvation they had received.

With hearts aflame and a resoluteness of spirit they went down into the street and proclaimed to the people the great things of God. The power of their proclamation was heard by those who had come from all over the Roman Empire to be part of the religious celebrations that were taking place. The newly empowered disciples' ministry that day, was such that three thousand souls were added to their number and came into the Kingdom of God.

The Incarnation had left the glory of His Father's Kingdom and became a man for one principal purpose, to undo the evil influences and effects that Satan had established in the life of so many people. Now through His sacrificial death and the power of His resurrection that work was moving wonderfully ahead. People confessed the sin in their lives, received forgiveness and embraced holiness and righteousness whilst bowing the knee to the Incarnation. As they did so

He received them into His Kingdom and gave them the gift of eternal life. The satanic power of death over them, which had held them in fear of death for so long, was now broken and declared null and void as Heaven's gates opened wide to receive them and the arms of a loving God embraced them.

The new life that the Incarnation's followers received had within it a critical spiritual factor that now came into effect. When a person bowed the knee to the Incarnation and made the decision to invite Him into their life so they became His disciple. The Holy Spirit became resident within them with their body becoming His temple. Now, they had the same Holy Spirit empowering as the Incarnation and the miraculous work that the Incarnation had demonstrated could continue through them.

The Holy Spirit continued His work and the Incarnation's disciples came to be known as, "The Followers of the Way," and they gossiped the good news of a restored life and eternal salvation to those around them. The movement grew with more and more people receiving the Holy Spirit's life transforming power. Within these groups the ministries of healing and deliverance, in which the Incarnation had trained His disciples, were functioning. The sick were healed, the lame walked, the blind saw, the deaf heard and those who were spiritually oppressed were cleansed. The number of His followers grew exponentially as these ministries were effective in people's lives.

Satan cursed the "The Followers of the Way" as their numbers grew, but he was most gratified by what he saw happening in the rest of human society. Slowly but surely a layer of deceit and corruption was being formed beneath the surface of human life as his demons went about their work. As time passed so Satan and his demons continued their nefarious work of temptation and corruption. They became well established in every strata of human society.

In opposition to them were the "The Followers of the Way." They had a dynamic certainty of life and ministry that was faith based; cutting edge, and risk centred. Their ministry's supernatural content reflected the dynamic power seen previously in the Incarnation's ministry.

Satan and his minions had done their nefarious work so well that he was sure the time had come for a knockout blow to be administered against the Incarnation's followers. Although he knew he was the ruler of the Earth he longed for the final destruction of everything and everyone that did not bow the knee to him. As he pondered this desire a heinous idea began to form in his mind and he realised that for his plan to be truly effective he must again take the form of the Great Red Dragon. His ability to do this flowed from the fact that he had the capacity to change his form at will and could even masquerade as an angel of light if he so desired.

To obtain maximum effect from the moment at which his transmogrification would occur he sent his messenger demons out across the Earth. They were ordered to proclaim that every one of his demons, from the lowliest apprentice, to the generals and field marshals and every rank in between, were to immediately assemble before him in the bowl of Insinticus, his favourite active volcano. He felt sure that here they would be away from the eyes and ears of angels.

They came in their thousands and tens of thousands, fallen spiritual beings of every imaginable size and description.

When all his forces had assembled on a ledge that cut deep into the wall of the volcano, several hundred feet above the molten lava pond, he left them there in the heat and the acidic fumes to await his arrival. When he felt that they had been punished enough for the transgressions against his will that had never come to his notice, but of which he was sure they were guilty, he condescended to appear before them and address them.

Standing with the red glow of molten lava illuminating his goat-like outline from behind, which made him appear to have a supernatural aura around him, he drew himself up to his full height and in a stentorian voice announced, **"You will all be aware that I have now established myself as the ruler of the world and that I am now, and will be forever more, the great, 'I am.' I am the master of this world and I rule and reign autonomously with regard for no one. My kingdom is everlasting and I am without end, I am eternal."**

He raised his forelegs and parried the air with his hoofs whilst thrusting his goat like head forward and striking upwards with his horns. He chose his moment well and being sure that every eye was focused upon him he instantly transmogrified into the Great Red Dragon. Satan achieved the result he was aiming for, as he heard every demon suck in air and gasp incredulously at what they saw happen before their eyes.

He was now enormous, many times larger than he had been in his goat like configuration. He raised his head high and blasted flames into the midst of his demons, instantly incinerating hundreds and setting fire to many more. As their screams came to his ears so his great tail flashed like lightning across the space separating him from his subordinates and sweeping away many from the front ranks off the ledge and into the molten lava beneath them. He roared obscenities into the air and cackled mirthlessly as he revelled in the destruction and level of fear he had created.

As the dark green and black smoke from his nostrils mingled with the sparks his internal combustion system was still creating, he bellowed at the assembly, *"I have the power of life and death over every one of you, do not forget that. I am to be obeyed without question for I am your Lord and Master and you will worship me!"*

Satan had already decided his next move in destroying all who were not part of his evil empire. He was determined to raise up a man who was full of sin and corruption deep within his character but externally appeared to be upright, honest and truthful. He had identified such a man knowing him to have political influence and excellent communication skills.

The man he had in mind was a very senior diplomat who was in good standing with the world's leaders, a charismatic figure who commanded international respect and also masqueraded as a "Follower of the Way."

What most people did not know, but which Satan knew, was that underneath his veneer of respectability this man was a warlock and a true Luciferian. The coven to which he belonged met regularly at night, in a clearing deep in a forest and dressed in black hooded gowns, they performed satanic rituals while standing within a pentagram marked out on the forest floor. They were regularly involved in human sacrifice and were all deeply committed to the worship of their Lord Satan.

A messenger demon, whose name was Envoyus, was responsible for keeping an eye on the coven's activities which came to Satan in the form of a monthly report. This recorded the regularity of their meetings and the principal depraved activities they entered into. Satan decided to be present at their next meeting.

It was a moonless night with a gentle breeze disturbing the uppermost branches of the trees. The coven was well into its heinous activities when Satan, the object of their worship arrived. From the light of a circle of lanterns set around the edge of the pentagram Satan was able to observe everything that was happening. On an altar positioned in the centre of the pentagram was a newly born baby which was to be sacrificed that night and its blood drunk by the coven's members.

The senior warlock present was the man that Satan had come to empower. After the sacrifice of the child had been made and the baby's blood consumed from a goblet, which was passed from person to person in the coven's circle, Satan made his presence known.

He came in his horned goat embodiment and materialised in their midst as they were offering a prayer to their Lord and Master for a further infilling of his demonic presence.

When they had recovered from the initial shock of Satan being with them, he spoke to them in a voice devoid of any emotion and which was emitted gruffly from deep in his chest, "I wholeheartedly receive your oblations and am pleased with your activities this night. Each of you will be eternally cursed, but in this life you will have wealth, fame and high social standing. I have come to empower for a special task, the man who is your leader."

As he finished speaking he moved across to where the object of his interest was standing, who immediately dropped to his knees, as Satan approached him. Laying his cloven forelegs on the man's head he spoke again, "Your heart is aligned with mine and I have come to commission you for a most important role. For you, I have appointed the special task of world leadership that will bring the people of the world under my complete control and into a greater depth of adulation to me. It will raise me to the pinnacle of their adoration and worship.

You are to be the Antichrist and I commission you as such. You will represent me before kings and princes, governors and politicians and your leadership of the world will come about as you bring together the nations into a time of peace. For three and a half years the people of the world will have a unity they have never known before and you will be feted and honoured. You will be called, 'The Great Peace Maker.'

At the end of that time your true character will be revealed and your loyalty to me, as my earthly representative, shall be seen by all. On my behalf, you shall declare yourself to be the God of this world and you shall be my instrument of persecution against "The Followers of the Way." They shall be given into your hands, that you might destroy them."

Leaning forward towards the man's head, Satan spat a globule of green and black slime onto his forehead and with his right foreleg shaped it into an upside down cross. Having completed what he came to do Satan spoke a curse over the entire coven and departed as quickly as he had come, leaving behind him a foul stench and a sooty trail.

After his ordination things moved quickly for the Antichrist as Satan's empowering worked within him and quickly shaped world events. Under the power of his satanic anointing, he spoke to world leaders travelling from country to country and capital to capital as they committed to his peace plan. The nations of the world came together under his charismatic leadership as wars, sectarian violence, racial disharmony, political disputes, terrorist activities and interpersonal hatreds came to an end. All the world was crying, "Peace, peace" and seeing the Antichrist as their saviour.

There were now many humans who had given themselves over to his satanic rule completely. He now issued an order for a group of them in every society in the world to create a large statue of a "Beast like Creature" that was to be worshipped by every human being on Earth. Arrayed behind each of the statues was a line of guillotines and anyone who refused to worship was to be instantly beheaded.

Those who did worship the statue of the Beast had the privilege of the insertion of a microchip into their right hand or under the skin of their forehead. The microchip contained each person's financial information; their bank account details, the value of investments, information concerning any stocks and shares they held and it gave them the ability to make financial transactions. Without the microchip it was impossible to buy and sell. A person could not purchase food, pay their mortgage, access medical services or supplies, put fuel in their vehicle, pay school fees, buy clothing or do any of the financial transactions that lubricate the life of a human being making it worthwhile.

If a person was of pensionable age their rights in that regard were also contained within the microchip as was their medical history. The microchip held the record of a person's life and gave them access to the necessities of life. All they had to do to obtain the microchip was to bow down and worship the Beast. Their lives being administered from that moment on by a One World Government under the control of the Antichrist.

The "Followers of the Way" were especially targeted. The Antichrist's administration had decreed that all religious activity must be registered. It was easy for them to be rounded up by the Religious Police and brought before the Beast's statue, to bow the knee in worship and pay homage to it.

This was the moment of truth for the Incarnation's followers and there were many of them. In every nation and of every tribe and tongue, men and women, young and old had moved from Satan's kingdom into the Kingdom of God. They were the saints whose commitment to the Incarnation was about to be tested. Throughout the world they were brought together and assembled in groups of twelve. This number was chosen because the Incarnation had had twelve disciples always close to Him. Now the closeness of each follower's relationship to Him was to be tested.

Before bringing each group before the statue of the Beast they were taken first to the execution area where the heads of those already slain were on spikes alongside each guillotine. The shed blood of those martyrs was left in the catching bowls of each guillotine for them to see. Then, they were taken to the statue nearby and asked the question, "Will you bow down and worship the Beast?" In some cases the answer was an instantaneous, "Yes," as the person apostatised giving away their commitment to the Incarnation and submitting themselves to the worship and rule of the Antichrist.

On these occasions it was not unusual for the statue to speak, outpouring from his mouth great proclamations concerning the supremacy and value of the Great Red Dragon and the Antichrist, to whom the Dragon had given power. Interspersed with these statements were blasphemies that denigrated the Incarnation and held Him up for ridicule.

The outworking of religion in a person's life, as opposed to a vital living faith, was being tested. In some cases the person's faith and spiritual values were found to be insufficient for entry into life eternal, as they made the decision to continue living their earthly life. As each of these apostasies occurred, there was waiting in the wings, a group of demons whose assignment was to spiritually embrace the convert and encourage them deeper into the satanic life. However, there were many who loved not, their life unto death, refused to worship the statue of the Beast and were executed.

One such person was a young man who had been healed of a pronounced stutter as a small group of the Incarnation's followers had ministered to him in healing prayer. He had experienced the power and presence of the Living God and had no intention of breaking the relationship that existed between him and the God he had come to love and serve.

As he was brought before the statue of the Beast and asked if he would bow down and worship he replied with an emphatic, ***"No, not now or ever!"*** He was led immediately to a guillotine and was forced to kneel under its blade. As he did so two magnificent warrior angels with their swords drawn stood either side of him, upholding him spiritually as he shouted in a loud voice, ***"My Lord and my God, into your hands I commend my spirit. You I will worship and adore always..."*** There his voice trailed off as the blade of the guillotine did its work. The two angels then escorted his soul into the fullness of the Father's Kingdom.

On another occasion a married couple refused to worship the Beast and as they knelt under the guillotines blades they held hands and encouraged each other not to apostasise, but to hold firm to their faith. They died with their fingers entwined and again the angels were there to escort their souls to Heaven.

Looking down from Heaven, the Father saw all that was happening and decided it was time He moved in power against what He saw.

The Father knew that the time had come for the Incarnation to return to the Earth, for He was aware that so many of the "Followers of the Way" had been praying for His second coming to occur and were eagerly awaiting Him now that the gospel had been preached to every nation on Earth.

Everyone in Heaven knew this was to be a cataclysmic event, the occurring of which was not to be foretold by a herald, as the Incarnation's first coming had been, but was to be sudden and without any pre-warning. It was to be a surprise to those who dwell in Heaven and to those who live on the Earth, expected and yet predetermined with its timing known only to the Father.

The Incarnation would not return as the Suffering Servant as He had come previously, but as the Lord of Heaven and Earth. Not in quietness and secrecy, but as a calamitous happening with His glory being seen in every part of the world simultaneously. Every eye will see and every ear will hear and there will be nobody on the Earth who is unaware of His majestic and holy presence descending before them. Everyone will bow the knee, such will the glory of His coming be. His transition from Heaven to Earth will be accompanied by magnificent angels, a cry of command, the voice of an archangel and the trumpet of God as it heralds His return.

Then, those who have died as a "Follower of the Way" will be awakened and be the first to ascend to meet Him. Following after them will be the "Followers of the Way", who are currently alive and they will join the Incarnation in the clouds, be reunited with Him and never be separated from Him again.

He spoke to the Archangel Michael, the captain of Heaven's armies, and asked him to select a mighty warrior angel for whom he had a special task. Michael could think of no one better than his friend Loyola and nominated him for the assignment. The Father took Loyola and Michael to one side and instructed them carefully in what He wanted them to do. He then placed the key to the bottomless pit and a great chain into Loyola's hand. Michael's role was to command a squadron of warrior angels and take them into combat against Satan's bodyguards to allow Loyola to get through to where Satan was and complete his task.

Satan had again transmogrified into the Great Red Dragon. He intended going to the execution area and using the flames from his mouth to torture those who were to die prior to them being beheaded. Before he could put this plan into action he saw above him a battle erupt. Michael's forces were dealing with Satan's Bodyguard Company, dividing them down the middle and pushing the two halves apart to allow Loyola to come through the centre of them on his way to Satan.

As Loyola descended to where Satan was, he whirled the great chain around his head and with absolute precision wound it around the Great Red Dragon, locking him into it and rendering him bound. Now pulling at the chain, he dragged Satan downwards towards the bottomless pit, whilst taking authority over him and commanding him to be bound spiritually as well as physically.

Down and down Loyola went, towing behind him the Great Red Dragon, bound not only by a great chain but also by spiritual power. The bottomless pit was now in front of him and using the key the Father had given him he unlocked it and cast Satan into it slamming the door shut, locking it and placing a seal upon it; which ensured it could not be opened for a thousand years.

During that thousand year period, the Father had a special role for those followers of the Incarnation who had been beheaded for refusing to worship the Beast and for not receiving the microchip into their forehead or upon their hand.

He brought them into the fullness of His Kingdom and seated them on thrones to honour them. There they reigned with the Incarnation as God's priests for the thousand year period.

As the thousand years came to an end the Father made the decision that Satan was to be released from the bottomless pit for a period of time. This was to test the people of the world, as the Great Deceiver came among them again. Would their integrity hold fast or would they become subject to his deception?

Upon his release from the bottomless pit Satan's rage at having been imprisoned, roared like an erupting volcano and he gathered together not only his spiritual demonic forces but also, from all over the world, those humans he had deceived and corrupted since his release. They came in their thousands; tens of thousands and unnumbered millions, bringing with them all the armaments they had accumulated. A mighty force equipped and motivated to make war upon and destroy every "Follower of the Way."

Satan's armies formed a formidable force with their field guns, mortars, flamethrowers, automatic weapons and innumerable soldiers they surrounded the Incarnation's followers within their city. With their weapons and superbly equipped troops they formed a ring of steel from which no one was going to escape.

Each army, with their field guns and other heavy weapons had been given their specific targets and their arcs of fire. Sights had been zeroed-in and high explosive shells loaded into the guns' breaches. The millions of foot soldiers were trained and ready and having been promised a large sum of money for every saint they killed, were strongly motivated for action with a blood lust crying out for satisfaction. Satan's demons were in position in the sky over the city providing Black Shield Cover and ready to do battle with Michael's warriors should they appear.

Militarily everything was ready and Satan had positioned himself on a hill overlooking the city. He had chosen a place of safety on an elevated position where he could observe everything that was to happen and also be seen by all his forces. In the sky immediately above him, were his bodyguards, he felt invulnerable and supreme with his black heart set on the destruction that would bring him final victory. He would give the signal for the battle to commence by raising his head and nostrils upward and blasting a column of fire into the sky which would be seen by his forces. Then hell on Earth would erupt as the big guns fired and the foot soldiers charged, the city would be destroyed and every "Follower of the Way" put to death.

All this he optimistically anticipated for he knew it would happen and that he and his armies were invincible. Now the moment had come for final victory and he raised his enormous head and pointing it skyward. He then sucked in a massive amount of air that would provide the combustion for the flame that would initiate his ultimate act of hatred, vengeance and destruction.

He paused, with his lungs full of air and the fire within him ready to ignite his inflammable material as his mind placed a final curse on his enemies, the Incarnation and His followers. He released the pressure in his lungs and as His internal combustion system was about to be activated so the Father commanded holy fire to come down from Heaven. The heat it produced was intense as it descended instantaneously upon all Satan's forces. Many of his troops were incinerated, the shells within their guns began exploding and boxes of ammunition detonated. The fire coming down from Heaven was now met by a sheet of flame coming up from exploding munitions. A scene of absolute carnage resulted as the heavenly fire caused massive explosions, blowing to smithereens significant portions of Satan's armies. Large weapons and boxes of munitions were blasted high into the air as they detonated and rained yet more burning and exploding material down upon Satan's troops. Many of his human forces died instantly with many more catching fire. The last sound that many of them made were their screams as they were incinerated. Fire was now everywhere as this blazing inferno raced through Heavens' enemies, igniting, exploding, consuming the oxygen and producing a devastating and catastrophic scene, as Satan's forces were annihilated and their destruction accomplished.

The only survivor, was Satan himself sitting high upon his hill. Again, Michael's Net Capture Company came into action, swooping down upon him and ensnaring him in a massive net. Then lifting him bodily, he was transported to a lake of fire into which he was cast in company with the Beast, both to be tormented for eternity. The final sound heard from them was their screams of agony as the flames enveloped them and a torment began that would never cease but last for ever and ever.

In the Kingdom of Heaven, the angels breathed a sigh of relief and congratulated one another on a task well done. The cleansing of the Earth is now complete and every demonic stronghold and influence destroyed along with the old Heaven and Earth. Human fallenness, satanic contamination and every person who bowed the knee to Satan and every fallen angel that sided with Lucifer has been dealt with. The Father's relationship with human beings is now fully restored, with holiness and righteousness reinstated throughout a newly created Heaven and Earth. There the love of God will reign supreme over all creation as the Kingdom of God in all its fullness is established upon the Earth.

The Incarnation's mission is now complete.

EPILOGUE

The book you have just read is clearly a work of fiction, but embedded in the imaginary are some very real spiritual truths. The principle characters, the Father, the Incarnation and Satan are absolute realities, as are the kingdoms over which they reign.

Humans are eternal beings and will spend eternity in one of two kingdoms, either Heaven or Hell. So it is most important that you understand that the choices you make will determine your eternal destiny. The Bible says:

> **Choose this day whom you will serve...**
> **as for me and my family we serve the Lord.**
>
> *Joshua 24: 15*

When the Father incarnated into the human race He did so as the man Jesus and you cannot enter the Father's Kingdom except through the Lord Jesus.

If you have not yet chosen to be part of the Father's Kingdom and genuinely desire to do so, then you are invited to pray the following prayer:

Father God, I understand that you incarnated into the human race and became the man Jesus.

Lord Jesus, I thank you for dying on the Cross for me that my sins might be forgiven and the way opened for me to spend eternity with you in the Father's Kingdom.

Lord Jesus, I receive you now as my Saviour and invite you to be the Lord of my life.

I ask you Lord Jesus to fill me with your Holy Spirit. Please empower me to become the person you designed and created me to be.

I pray this in the name of Jesus, my Saviour and Lord. Amen.

If you have responded by sincerely praying this prayer you are invited to email us at brian@charisma.org.nz to enable us to pray for you and uphold you in prayer.

BRIAN FRANCE

ABOUT THE AUTHOR

As a Platoon Commander during "The Troubles" in Northern Ireland, Brian was badly injured when 15lbs of high explosive detonated a metre behind him. Miraculously healed by prayer, he is now the Director of Charisma Christian Ministries in Auckland, New Zealand.

Brian's story is featured in the book, Radical Lives 1 by Janet Balcombe. An excerpt:

BRIAN FRANCE

An Irish bombshell with the power of God

The Royal Air Force Regiment had been deployed in Northern Ireland as part of the peacekeeping forces for some years and this was Brian's third tour of duty. He was now responsible for the security of the Walled City of Londonderry. It was early March, the weather was cold and damp, and his men were on the streets providing both mobile and standing patrols. As unexploded bombs were discovered, his men cordoned off the area and called the Bomb Disposal Squad. In dealing with the aftermath of bomb explosions they did what they could for the injured, and kept people from entering damaged buildings. Five bombs had already gone off when Brian was alerted to bomb number six, an unexploded bomb, by a radio message from the Control Centre.

> "It took a second or two for me to realise that the shop I was standing in had a bomb planted there ready to explode. I turned to my left and was going to shout, *"Get out!"* to my senior sergeant who was coming in behind me. I never quite got those words out as at that instant an estimated fifteen pounds of high explosive went off a metre behind me."

In a flash, his entire world was dominated by the exploding bomb as the sound of it momentarily became his whole existence. The detonation completely demolished the room, stripping the linings off the walls, bringing down the ceiling and blasting a large hole in the floor. It picked Brian up in its destructive grip, doing it's best to destroy him as he was hurled out the front of the bakery, along with a mass of debris...

To purchase *Radical Lives 1* with Brian's story of survival and miraculous healing, visit wildsidepublishing.com/buy-books/radical-lives-1

To purchase more copies of *Clash of the Kingdoms*, and to read Brian's latest blog, visit brianfrance.co.nz

Healing and deliverance meetings with Brian France and Charisma Christian Ministries team, are held every Tuesday evening from 7pm to 9pm (unless postponed), at the Salvation Army Centre, 18 Allright Place, Mt Wellington, Auckland.

One-day seminars on healing and deliverance are also held. Email brian@charisma.org.nz for details.

Visit charisma.org.nz

9 780473 505639